"It's me, all right!"

He must have been staring, because Sherry flashed him an embarrassed grin. At least, he thought it was Sherry. He couldn't get any words past his lips. She looked nice, he supposed, but she didn't look like Sherry anymore. Gone was the cascade of curls that had reached the middle of her back. Now her hair fell in gentle waves down to her shoulders—and it was brown.

But the changes didn't stop there. What had happened to those glossy red lips? Her clothes could only be described as sedate, and her shoes had no heel whatsoever. Even her voice seemed more subdued.

With an inward groan, he realized this metamorphosis was his doing. She'd changed for him....

Dear Reader,

Things get off to a great start this month with another wonderful installment in Cathy Gillen Thacker's series THE DEVERAUX LEGACY. In *Their Instant Baby*, a couple comes together to take care of an adorable infant—and must fight *their* instant attraction. Be sure to look for a brand-new Deveraux story from Cathy when *The Heiress*, a Harlequin single title, is released next March.

Judy Christenberry is also up this month with a story readers have been anxiously awaiting. Yes, Russ Randall does finally get his happy ending in *Randall Wedding*, part of the BRIDES FOR BROTHERS series. We also have *Sassy Cinderella* from Kara Lennox, the concluding story in her memorable series HOW TO MARRY A HARDISON. And rounding out things is *Montana Miracle*, a stranded story with a twist from perennial favorite Mary Anne Wilson.

Next month begins a yearlong celebration as Harlequin American Romance commemorates its twentieth anniversary! We'll have tons of your favorite authors with more of their dynamic stories. And we're also launching a brand-new continuity called MILLIONAIRE, MONTANA that is guaranteed to please. Plus, be on the lookout for details of our fabulous and exciting contest!

Enjoy all we have to offer and come back next month to help us celebrate twenty years of home, heart and happiness!

Sincerely,

Melissa Jeglinski
Associate Senior Editor
Harlequin American Romance

SASSY CINDERELLA
Kara Lennox

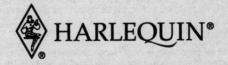

HARLEQUIN®

TORONTO • NEW YORK • LONDON
AMSTERDAM • PARIS • SYDNEY • HAMBURG
STOCKHOLM • ATHENS • TOKYO • MILAN • MADRID
PRAGUE • WARSAW • BUDAPEST • AUCKLAND

ISBN 0-373-16951-5

SASSY CINDERELLA

ABOUT THE AUTHOR

Texas native Kara Lennox has been an art director, typesetter, advertising copy writer, textbook editor and reporter. She's worked in a boutique, a health club and has conducted telephone surveys. She's been an antiques dealer and briefly ran a clipping service. But no work has made her happier than writing romance novels.

When Kara isn't writing, she indulges in an ever-changing array of weird hobbies, from rock climbing to crystal digging. But her mind is never far from her stories. Just about anything can send her running to her computer to jot down a new idea for some future novel.

Books by Kara Lennox

HARLEQUIN AMERICAN ROMANCE

Don't miss any of our special offers. Write to us at the following address for information on our newest releases.

Harlequin Reader Service
U.S.: 3010 Walden Ave., P.O. Box 1325, Buffalo, NY 14269
Canadian: P.O. Box 609, Fort Erie, Ont. L2A 5X3

HARDISON FAMILY TREE

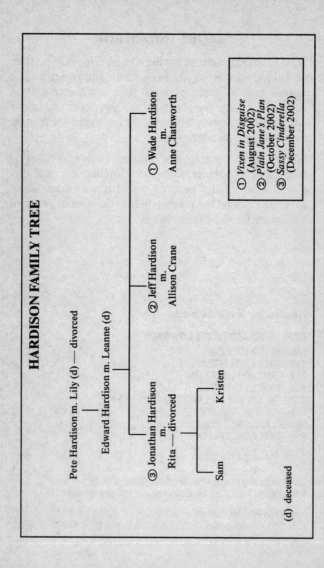

Pete Hardison m. Lily (d) — divorced

Edward Hardison m. Leanne (d)

③ Jonathan Hardison
m.
Rita — divorced

② Jeff Hardison
m.
Allison Crane

① Wade Hardison
m.
Anne Chatsworth

Sam   Kristen

(d) deceased

① *Vixen in Disguise*
(August 2002)
② *Plain Jane's Plan*
(October 2002)
③ *Sassy Cinderella*
(December 2002)

Chapter One

He had no idea how it had happened. One minute he was herding a bunch of cows to their winter pasture. The next, Jonathan Hardison was flying through the air, landing on his head with a thud hard enough to knock the air out of him, then being stomped on by the same stupid horse that had just bucked him off.

Damn, being stomped on hurt. A white-hot pain stabbed through his leg, but he was no stranger to pain. Ranching wasn't an occupation for any guy who couldn't stand the sight of blood or who got the vapors if he cut his hand on barbed wire.

As he lay there on the ground, struggling to get a breath, his right-hand man got off his horse and came over to check out the damages. Cal Chandler was a new man at the Hardison Ranch, but he was the local veterinarian's grandson, and he seemed competent enough.

Until now.

Cal just stared at Jonathan, gaping.

"Well, don't just stand there," Jonathan said when he could finally catch enough breath to speak. "Help me up."

"I don't think so, boss," Cal said in a shaky voice. He waved away Jon's horse, which had come over to investigate why his master was on the ground, having apparently forgotten that moments ago he was in a blind, bucking panic. "I think you better just stay right there till an ambulance gets here."

"What? Have you gone loco? I might be a little banged up…" Jonathan leaned up on one elbow, then wished he hadn't because he got a good look at his leg. It was bent in a place no leg should be bent.

"You got a cell phone on you?" Cal asked.

"In the saddlebag," Jon said, just before he passed out.

"It isn't as bad as it could have been," said Jeff, Jonathan's brother, the next day at Mother Frances Hospital in Tyler, Texas. Tyler was the closest big town to the Hardison Ranch. "It was an ugly break, but at least the swelling's down."

"So let me go home," Jon grumbled. Lying in bed doing nothing was not his favorite way to spend time.

"Tomorrow. Maybe," Jeff said. "I'm more worried about the concussion than the leg, to tell you the truth." Jeff also happened to be Jonathan's doctor, and he seemed to love bossing his older brother around.

"Like hell, 'maybe,'" Jonathan said. "I'll check my own damn self out."

"Ohh, surly, are we?" Jeff's fiancée, Allison, had also dropped in for a visit, as if this was some kind of social event. Allison's presence was the only thing that kept Jonathan from cussing Jeff out.

"You'd be surly, too, if you had to wear one of these stupid gowns with your butt hanging out."

"Seriously, Jon," Allison said, "you shouldn't go home until you're sure you can handle it. You'll be on crutches—"

"No way. Put one of those rubber tips on this thing," Jonathan said, knocking his knuckles against his cast. "I can walk."

"You can*not* walk," Jeff said. "You put weight on this leg at this stage, it'll never heal."

"Then give me the crutches and let me get out of here."

"Maybe," Jeff said again. That word was starting to tick Jonathan off.

"Even with crutches, you're going to need some help when you go home," Allison said. "You've got two lively kids to care for."

"Pete can handle the kids," Jonathan said, referring to their eighty-one-year-old grandfather. Pete had built the Hardison Ranch from nothing, but he'd long ago deeded the property to his three grandsons and retired. He still lived in the house, though, and he helped take care of Jonathan's children: eight-year-old Sam and seven-year-old Kristin. He said it made him feel useful, which was just fine with Jonathan, since he'd been long divorced and needed help at home.

"You're forgetting," Jeff said. "Pete and Sally are getting married this Saturday."

"Ah, hell, that's right," Jonathan said. After the wedding, Pete and his long-time sweetheart, Sally Enderlin, were going on a weeklong cruise. "I don't care. I'll manage somehow.'' But he really didn't know how. His youngest brother, Wade, who ran a horse-breeding operation on his portion of the ranch, had offered to pitch in with the cattle-ranching work during Jonathan's recuperation. But how in the world would Jon cook, clean and supervise his superactive kids?

''I'll hire someone to come in,'' Jonathan said decisively.

But Jeff was shaking his head. ''You'll need someone there all the time, at least for the first week or so.''

Jonathan looked to Allison, half hoping she'd volunteer. But realistically he knew she couldn't. She was the dentist in Cottonwood, the small town where they all lived, and she had a thriving practice to manage. She couldn't just take off a week.

Allison had a peculiar look on her face that Jonathan had come to associate with an impending brainstorm.

''What are you thinking?'' he asked her pointblank.

''I have this friend in Dallas who's a nurse,'' Allison said, casting worried glances at Jeff. ''She's starting a new job in December, but for now she's at loose ends. I've been trying to get her to come visit me in Cottonwood. If she knew someone here needed her nursing skills, she'd be here in a flash.''

''I do not need a nursemaid,'' Jonathan protested, picturing some horse-faced pain queen with a hypodermic.

''But that's precisely what you *do* need,'' Jeff said.

"I'd feel much better about releasing you if I knew a registered nurse was keeping an eye on you. Why don't you call her, Allie?"

Allison looked at Jonathan. "It's up to you."

He saw no other alternative. Once this nurse saw he could take care of himself, she would leave him alone and focus on caring for the children. He nodded his assent.

Allison smiled and opened her purse. "I'll call Sherry right now."

Jeff's jaw dropped. "Sherry? You mean Sherry McCormick, the she shark?"

"Oh, Jeff, you're way too harsh. So, she had a crush on you. So what?" Allison scrolled through the phone numbers on her cell phone.

"A crush? She wanted to eat me alive at that convention."

This was getting interesting, Jonathan thought. A she shark? Didn't sound like a horse face, at least.

"She happens to be an excellent nurse," Allison said. "At least, she just landed a job working for one of Dallas's top cosmetic surgeons."

"You can't bring Sherry McCormick to Cottonwood," Jeff said flatly. "A city girl like her won't fit in here."

"What's the matter? You afraid she'll come after you again? Well, don't. She's over you."

"And you want to inflict her on Jonathan instead?"

Allison waved away Jeff's concern. "Jonathan isn't her type. Anyway, she told me she never gets involved with a patient. It isn't professional."

"Why am I not her type?" Jonathan wanted to

know. Unfortunately, this Sherry sounded like *his* type—flashy and aggressive. His ex-wife, Rita, had been exactly that, all spike heels and expensive perfume. It had not been a match made in heaven. Rita had about died of boredom in tiny Cottonwood, Texas, and not even her two children had been enough to make her stick around. She'd fled to New Orleans, where she'd grown up, and saw the kids maybe twice a year.

"She goes for doctors and lawyers," Jeff answered. "Guys in suits with expensive cars who will keep her on a steady diet of four-star restaurants and adorn her with diamonds."

That certainly didn't describe Jonathan.

"I'm not interested in romantic potential," Jonathan said. "If she's willing to come and can do the job, bring her on."

Allison flashed a satisfied smile and dialed a number on her cell phone. Jeff groaned.

SHERRY MCCORMICK drove slowly around the town square of Cottonwood, hardly believing her eyes. It could have been a set from a Hollywood back lot—for a period piece from the 1920s. *Quaint* hardly began to describe this town.

Fortunately, Sherry was a sucker for quaint. The picturesque shops and restaurants charmed her silly. Did people really live like that? Even as she tried to tell herself the idea of residing in the sticks repulsed her, she felt an insistent pull toward this place.

Cottonwood was a town a person could call home. Sherry had never lived in a place that felt like home. Certainly the double-wide in which she'd grown up hadn't qualified. Her parents had been a lot more interested in drinking and smoking dope than raising their only child—except to sporadically hurl criticism and occasional pieces of furniture her way. That was their idea of parenting.

She was okay with her current home, a condo in Dallas she'd bought last year. She'd taken great care in decorating it, choosing each picture and accent piece one at a time. But no matter how many homey touches she added, it still felt cold to her. She supposed no place could feel really like a home when only one person lived there.

But maybe that was her lot in life. She sighed as she turned her car away from town and followed the directions Allison had given her to the Hardison Ranch. She'd tried really hard to find a companion, a man she was compatible with, one who would love her, one who wanted to commit and eventually grow old with her. But it seemed the harder she tried, the worse things turned out. She'd found plenty of men who would love her—for one night. Maybe she just wasn't the kind of woman a man wanted hanging around for the rest of his life.

As sobering as that thought was, Sherry knew she could live without a husband. Growing old without children, though—she wasn't going to settle for that. Still, at thirty-one, she had a little time. And until she figured out the rest of her life, she had her nursing career, which was a real blessing. She'd been let go from her last position, an event that seemed grossly unfair to Sherry. She was a good nurse, a conscientious one, and it was only a personality conflict that had gotten her fired. But then she'd landed a plum position with the best plastic surgeon in Dallas, along with a big hike in pay, so it had all worked out.

Even this chance to come to Cottonwood and take care of an injured rancher had come at the right time, convincing her that nursing was where she needed to focus her energies. Her new job didn't start until next month and her finances were getting a little tight. The money she would earn as a live-in caregiver would help with some of those credit card bills she was using as a stopgap measure.

The Hardison Ranch was easy to find. She just had to follow what seemed like miles of white rail fences until she reached the main gate, which featured a hand-painted sign and a metal sculpture of a bucking longhorn cow. Or was it a bull? A steer? Whatever. Sherry knew nothing about cattle, and she didn't want to.

She turned her Firebird right and through the gate, rumbling over a cattle guard, then down a long, red dirt drive. She noticed a picturesque red barn off to her right. It looked like the model for countless amateur oil paintings.

"What a trip," she murmured aloud.

When the ranch house came into view, Sherry was impressed. It was a huge, rambling one-story building done in a pseudo log-cabin style. Pastures surrounded it on all sides, but a few trees had been spared to give the house shade from the hot Texas sun. Someone had planted chrysanthemums in front, which were covered in orange blossoms.

The house and grounds looked well maintained, and the few cows she saw in the distance grazed contentedly. She hoped the inside was as nice, but she had her doubts since from what Allison had told her, the Hardison Ranch was a bastion of male bachelorhood. She didn't relish the thought of devoting all her time to scrubbing floors and toilets, but that was what she would do if she had to. When she'd left the trailer park, she'd sworn she would never live anyplace dirty again, not even temporarily.

Sherry pulled her Firebird next to a pickup truck. Several other vehicles were parked in the drive, all of them trucks or SUVs. Her little red sports car looked out of place, she thought with a grin, wondering what her new employer would think of it.

She hadn't given much thought to her boss and patient, Jonathan Hardison. When she'd asked Allison if Jonathan was as cute as his younger brother, her friend had been cagey with her answer, saying, "He's handsome enough when he smiles, which isn't very often." Sherry figured that was fair warning that Jonathan wouldn't be an easy customer.

Well, soon she'd know exactly what the situation was. She couldn't sit here in the car all day. She applied a fresh coat of lipstick, powdered her nose, fluffed her blond hair, grabbed her overnight case from the passenger seat, and got out of the car.

"SHE'S HERE!" announced Sam, Jonathan's eight-year-old son, who peered excitedly out the living room window.

"I wanna see!" Jon's seven-year-old, Kristin, raced to the window to join her brother.

If Jonathan could have done the same, he would have. But he was stuck in a recliner, his leg elevated on pillows. He could move, even walk with the aid of crutches when he had to, but Jeff had ordered him to stay put unless absolutely necessary.

For once, Jonathan had listened to his brother. Now that he was off those nice painkilling drugs they'd given him at the hospital, the leg hurt—a lot. He would do whatever it took to heal the fracture as quickly as he could so he could get back to work. If that meant acting like an invalid for a few days, he'd do it.

His whole family had come to the hospital this morning to take him home, like it was some kind of party. Now they were crawling all over the house. Jeff and their father, Edward Hardison, who was also a doctor, were here to instruct Jonathan's new nurse on his care. Wade was here ostensibly because he was running the ranch for the next couple of weeks, but Jonathan suspected Wade and his wife, Anne, were hanging around because they were curious about the new nurse.

Allison was also there to greet Sherry because she'd arranged the whole thing. Gregarious Sally, Pete's fiancée, didn't really have an excuse for being here, except that she and Pete were seldom apart these days. They'd all been fussing around him like old women, fixing up a guest room, doing laundry, stocking the pantry. Much as he loved his family, Jonathan wished they would all just go away and leave him in peace. He could work things out with the nursemaid himself.

Wade joined the kids at the window and let out a low whistle. ''Allison, are you nuts? She doesn't even look like a nurse. She looks like a—''

''Don't say it.'' Allison held up her hand to halt her future-brother-in-law's tirade. ''You can't judge a book by its cover. Haven't you ever heard that?''

Like a what? Jonathan wanted to know.

''Let's have a look at her,'' said Pete, Jonathan's wiry grandfather, toddling over to the living room window and peeking around the edge of the curtain. ''She can't be that—holy moly, that's some hunk of woman.''

''Pete, really,'' Allison admonished. ''Sherry is… an individual. She has her own unique sense of style.''

''Yeah, kind of trashy chic,'' added Anne, who was peeking through the shades from a different window. ''My gosh, get a load of that car!''

''Get a load of those spike heels,'' Wade added.

''She's wearing leopard-skin pants!'' Sam observed.

''For pity's sake,'' Jonathan said, ''the woman's going to think we're a bunch of weirdos, peering at people through cracks in the curtains.'' But his mind was focused on the comment—*some hunk of woman…trashy chic…spike heels…leopard-skin pants*. He was undoubtedly intrigued. Did that mean big hair and tight clothes? His heart beat a little faster at the thought even as he told himself to knock it off.

The last thing he needed was to develop a crush on some fast-talking city girl.

The doorbell rang, and Allison gave an exasperated sigh. "Anyone else want to take a verbal shot at poor Sherry before I let her in? 'Cause I promise you, first person who says anything mean to her face, I'll kick 'em clean to the Gulf of Mexico."

As Allison opened the door, Jonathan pretended to find great interest in the *TV Guide*. Everyone else could make a big to-do over Sherry. He intended for her to know she'd been allowed here under protest. Agreeing to the nurse was the only way he could get Jeff to discharge him from the hospital.

"Allie, honey, you look fabulous!" The newcomer stepped through the door and enveloped Allison in a hug. "Being engaged must agree with you. Jeff, you rascal, it's about time someone made an honest man out of you." She kissed Jeff on the cheek.

Jonathan watched all this from the corner of his eye, getting only an impression of a slender body topped with a huge cloud of blond hair. He was dying to get a good look at her, but he didn't want to be caught staring. And he had this niggling suspicion that he would want to stare.

Allison introduced Sherry to the rest of the crowd, including the children, who had suddenly gone mute.

Finally Jonathan couldn't put it off. Allison was leading Sherry to his corner of the room. He looked up from the *TV Guide* and assumed a smile, which immediately froze on his face. Standing before him was the most fantastic creature he'd ever laid eyes on, a cross between Florence Nightingale and Madonna.

"Jonathan, this is Sherry McCormick," Allison was saying. Jonathan was only vaguely aware of what anyone said, however, as a buzz had started in his head, drowning out everything else.

Sherry held out her hand. Her fingers were tipped with inch-long, peach nails that exactly matched her lipstick. "Nice to meet you, Jonathan. I hope I can be a big help to you."

Her voice was high-pitched and breathy, kind of like Marilyn Monroe's. Jonathan took her hand, which felt cool and soft against his. He squeezed it briefly and murmured some pleasantry.

This was his nurse? He could more easily picture her sashaying down a runway than pushing a wheelchair down a hospital corridor. But she was a friend of Allison's, and she had a sincere-looking smile, so he supposed he had to trust that she had some idea of how to take care of people.

"So how did you manage to do this to yourself?" Sherry asked, indicating the full-leg fiberglass cast.

Jonathan didn't want to talk about his accident. He hadn't been bucked from a horse for a good many years, and it was an embarrassment that he'd let his normally placid gelding get the best of him.

"Sheer stupidity," he finally answered, hoping it would quell her curiosity.

"Let me show you to your room," Allison said. She looked at the small case Sherry held in her left hand. "You brought more luggage than that, right?"

"Oh, lots more," Sherry replied. "I don't travel light."

"If you'll give me your keys," Jeff said, "I'll bring your stuff in from the car."

Sherry obliged him, then allowed Allison to lead her down a hallway to the bedrooms. The children, who'd been staring at Sherry as if she were some exotic animal at the zoo, trailed after the two women. "You're right across the hall from Jonathan," Allison was saying as their voices faded away.

"Holy cow," Pete said, stifling a laugh.

"She's…different," said Edward, who made a show of mopping his round face with his handkerchief.

"Jeff warned us Sherry was flamboyant," Wade said, grinning ear to ear. "But nothing could have prepared me for the reality. She's kind of…"

"Kind of what?" Anne asked in a teasing voice as she joined Wade on the couch, leaning her head on his shoulder. "Last I checked, you *liked* big hair and tight clothes."

Wade's face turned ruddy. "Not for a nurse," he murmured, though he and Anne shared an understanding look. Anne, who was normally a sedate, conservative attorney, had first caught Wade's eye by decking herself out like a country-western singer, complete with sequins, and brazenly flirting with him at a rodeo.

Edward fixed his oldest son with a penetrating stare. "You're awfully quiet about all this. What do you think of her? Are you comfortable with her taking care of you and the kids?"

Comfortable? Not likely, when he had an arousal like a steel bar pushing against his jeans.

He shrugged, trying to look indifferent. ''I'm sure she'll be fine, and if she's not, I'll send her packing.'' He fervently hoped she would be a terrible nurse, and that he would find ten excuses before nightfall to fire her. Because otherwise he was going to have to work to keep his hands off her.

Chapter Two

Sherry struggled to breathe normally as Allison took her on a tour of the house. Though no women had inhabited this house for many years, it was neat and clean as a convent, calming her earlier fears. Which was good, because she had plenty of new concerns—like how she was going to remain a detached caregiver while caring for the most gorgeous man she'd ever laid eyes on.

She'd only been teasing Allison when she'd asked if Jonathan was good-looking. Normally she didn't care what her patients looked like, only that they needed her. She'd figured that if he was related to Jeff, who was movie-star handsome, he wouldn't be a gargoyle. But nothing had prepared her for exactly how good-looking the older brother would be—and very different from Jeff.

He was taller, for one thing. Sherry could tell even though Jonathan had been in a recliner. He was rangier, too—a bit broader in the shoulders, more sinewy, like a cowboy from those old cigarette billboards. His face still held on to its summer tan, though it was almost winter. His dark, wavy hair, a little unruly, was nothing like Jeff's sun-burnished locks. But it was the eyes that really caught Sherry in a snare. Dark, mysterious, wary. Nothing tickled her libido faster than a man with secrets to hide.

Unfortunately, her policy was strictly hands-off when it came to her patients. What a bummer. Why couldn't a guy like him show up in her life when she could actually take advantage?

Well, she might not be here that long, she reminded herself. The man's superficial smile hadn't extended to his eyes. Jonathan Hardison didn't want her in his house.

She didn't always make a great first impression. That was something she'd learned early, though she'd never understood why it was true. She always tried to be her most pleasant when she met new people.

At least most people liked her when they got to know her. Jonathan's resistance made her just that much more determined to win him over—if he didn't fire her first.

As for the kids, they were so precious they made her heart ache. All children made her feel that way, bringing back memories she'd just as soon keep buried. She liked to think she would be good with children, but in reality she hadn't spent enough time around any to know. She imagined she could keep them safe, clean and fed, which was the minimum this job required. But she wasn't sure if they would like her. For all she knew, they might believe she was trying to replace their mother.

"We laid in some groceries earlier today," Allison was explaining as they entered the kitchen. "I have no idea what you like to cook, so I bought some staples and also frozen convenience stuff, just in case. The ranch has an account at the grocery store, so you can just charge whatever you want.''

Sherry inspected the cupboards and refrigerator contents in the large, homey kitchen. There seemed to be plenty of everything she would need for several days. ''Will I need to get some sort of authorization?''

Allison looked at her blankly. ''For what?''

''To charge the groceries.''

Allison laughed. ''That's not necessary. I just called Clem down at Grubbs' Food Mart and let him know it's okay for you to sign on the Hardison account.''

Wow. That was small-town life, Sherry guessed. Everyone knew everyone and trusted everyone, apparently. Sherry wasn't sure how she felt about that. She was accustomed to the anonymity of the big city. She met new people every day and none of them could judge her on her past, only on what she let them see.

Sometimes that was enough, she conceded with a grin.

''Why are you smiling?'' the little girl asked.

Sherry's grin grew. ''Because I'm happy to be here, I guess. Sometimes I just smile for the heck of it. You know, doctors have done tests on people that prove smiling makes you happy, even if you aren't happy to start with.''

''That sounds like hogwash,'' the boy said as he peered hopefully into an empty cookie jar.

Sam, Sherry reminded herself. *Sam and Kristin.* She prided herself on remembering names because she'd learned that her patients felt more relaxed when she related to them as people, one on one.

"Sam!" Allison scolded. "That wasn't very nice."

"He just says that word because Grandpa Pete says it and he thinks it's funny," Kristin said. Then she turned shy blue eyes on Sherry. "You have pretty teeth."

"Best teeth money can buy," Sherry quipped.

Allison started to say something, then stopped.

"What?" Sherry prompted.

"I was just wondering what happened to your real teeth, because I'm a dentist and therefore unnaturally interested in people's mouths. But it's a rude question."

"No, it's not," Sherry said. "I chipped two of them by falling off a bicycle when I was a kid." That was the story she'd been using for a long time. It was a lot nicer than the truth.

"Well, someone did an excellent job on your caps," Allison said as they headed back through the dining room and into the living room. "Only a dentist like me would notice you *have* caps."

"Thanks." Getting her teeth fixed was one of the first things Sherry had attended to after she got out of nursing school.

Jeff was just coming through the front door with Sherry's luggage. It hadn't seemed like so much when she'd stuffed it all into the trunk and back seat of the Firebird, but now it looked like a tapestry-printed mountain growing in the middle of the room.

Jonathan frowned at the vast pile of luggage. Then he turned to Sherry. "You *are* here just for a few days, right?"

"I know it looks like a lot," Sherry said apologetically. "I never have been good at packing. Don't worry, the bags will be out of your way in a jiffy." She grabbed up as many of the smaller bags as she could carry and lugged them toward her room. Jeff and Allison got the rest.

"This room is really nice," Sherry said, running a finger along the top of the oak dresser. The comforter on the queen-size bed looked fluffy and warm, and there were at least four pillows, all with matching pillow slips.

"Anne made it over," Allison said. "She has really good taste. In fact, Anne is the one who made *me* over."

Allison had told Sherry the whole story when they first became friends. She'd wanted to catch Jeff's eye, so she'd done a radical makeover on herself, only to have Jeff fail to notice. He'd finally come to his senses and realized he loved Allison, but apparently his feelings had little to do with her appearance.

"Want me to help you unpack?" Allison asked.

"I'll do that later. Right now, I'd like to sit down with Jeff and learn more about Jonathan's medical condition to find out exactly what sort of care you want me to provide." She slipped a notebook and pen from the outer pocket of one of her bags.

"He has a concussion," Jeff said. "He landed on his head."

"I'm surprised he didn't leave a dent in the

ground," Allison said, "instead of the other way round."

"Of the two, his head's probably harder," Jeff agreed. "Anyway, Sherry, Jonathan also has an angulated, displaced fracture of the tibia, but it was simple. There were no bone fragments, so the orthopedist didn't feel surgery was necessary, just reduction and a cast. But there was a lot of swelling and bruising, so he needs to keep the leg elevated—and keep off it, of course. Otherwise, just watch for signs of infection. He has some minor abrasions where the horse kicked him."

Sherry gasped. "A horse kicked him?"

"After bucking him off," Allison added. "These men and their horses... Well, anyway, other than keeping an eye on Jonathan, you'll just need to cook and clean and help out with the kids. I know it's not a job that requires your level of skill—"

"Oh, I don't mind," Sherry said quickly, then realized how overeager she sounded. But the idea of playing house with Jonathan Hardison and his family was far more appealing than it should have been. "Is Jonathan on any medication?"

"Antibiotics and Vicadin for pain, but he's not taking the pain pill. He said he didn't like how it made him groggy." Jeff pulled two prescription bottles out of his shirt pocket and handed them to Sherry. "Make him take the Vicadin if the pain keeps him awake at night. He needs to sleep if he wants to heal."

"Gotcha." She scribbled in her notebook as they all three returned to the living room.

"Kristin has food allergies," Allison added. "The list of everything she's allergic to is on the fridge."

More scribbles in the notebook.

"Sam hates baths and will go to any lengths to avoid them," Allison said with a chuckle. "Don't let him con you."

Sherry started to worry. What other idiosyncrasies did this family have, and what would they forget to tell her? She'd never done private-practice nursing before. She'd always worked in a hospital or doctor's office, where there were plenty of people around if she had any questions or problems.

"Why doesn't everybody stay for dinner?" Sherry asked. "I can make a Frito-chili pie that's out of this world."

JONATHAN COULDN'T BELIEVE his ears. The woman had been in his house for, what, fifteen minutes? And already she acted like she owned the place, inviting people to dinner. He wanted everyone to go home. He was in no shape to entertain guests.

At least he wouldn't have to go to the table. He planned to take his meals right here on a TV tray.

But the aggravating woman messed up those plans, too. Realizing Jonathan would have to eat his dinner alone if everyone else sat in the dining room, she announced she would serve dinner in the living room. "The kids can sit on the floor in front of the coffee table and everyone else can eat on TV trays. You have TV trays, right?" She looked at Jonathan.

He was forced to smile and tell her where the trays were kept.

Frito-chili pie. Jonathan knew it was a Texas tradition, but he wasn't fond of Mexican food of any kind. He liked his meat and potatoes. But the smell coming from the kitchen as Sherry cooked wasn't too bad.

Allison got out the trays, and Kristin helped her set places for everyone. Anne put some lively zydeco music on the CD player, while Sally turned on every light and lamp in the house. Pretty soon it was like a party.

A party was the last thing Jonathan needed. Couldn't his family see that? And Sherry—didn't she know injured people needed peace and quiet? What kind of nurse was she?

In less than an hour she had dinner ready. He had to give her credit for efficiency. The steaming square of casserole on his plate didn't cheer him, though. He would have preferred a nice pork chop.

"Do you normally have a blessing?" Sherry asked as everyone got settled in with their plates and drinks.

"Usually only when my father's here," Allison said. "I think I told you before, he's a minister. I suppose we should bless the meal. Would you like to do it, Sherry?"

"Oh, um, sure." She bowed her head. Jonathan would have done the same, but he was too entranced watching how Sherry's curls fell over one shoulder and breast, the very end teasing her cleavage. "Thank you, Lord, for this food," she said, "and for giving me a temporary job so the credit card companies don't come get me, and for Jonathan being on the road to a full recovery."

"Amen."

"Let's eat!" Sam said, picking up his fork and digging in. Everyone else followed suit.

From his first bite, Jonathan thought his mouth had caught fire. He somehow managed to swallow, chasing the bite down with a gulp of milk, but he coughed afterward. Looking around, he noticed he wasn't the only one experiencing difficulty with the meal. Jeff's eyes were watering, Edward had covered his mouth with his hand and his eyes were bulging, and Anne was gasping for breath.

Kristin was less polite. She spit out her first bite. "This is too hot!" she announced.

"No kidding," Sam said, staring at his food as if it were a poisonous snake.

Sherry looked at the children with concern. "Is it? I put peppers in the pie—I found them in the fridge, so I figured you wouldn't mind."

Pete chuckled. "Those're my peppers. I put 'em on everything, but these other tenderfoots don't like 'em." Pete took a second bite of the casserole, obviously not bothered by the piquant flavor.

"Daddy, can I have a peanut butter sandwich?" Kristin asked.

One by one everyone except Pete and Sherry found an alternate dinner. They tried to tell Sherry it wasn't her fault, but she was obviously embarrassed.

"What about you, Jonathan?" she asked. "Can I fix you something else?"

"I'm really not hungry," he announced. "I think I'll just go to bed."

Sherry dropped the sponge she was using to clean spills off the coffee table. "I'll help you."

He held up a hand to halt her approach. "I can manage, thanks." But, to his humiliation, he couldn't. He was stuck in the recliner.

Ignoring his objections, Sherry went to work levering him out of the chair, helping him balance on his good leg while he situated the crutches.

"I've got it now, thanks."

But the infernal woman hovered over him as he limped toward his room. "It's always hardest the first day on crutches," she said. "You'll get the hang of using them soon. Of course, you shouldn't walk much at all these first few days."

"I don't plan to—what in the name of all that's holy is that thing?" Jonathan stopped at the doorway to his bedroom, staring at this monstrous flowered balloon-looking thing on his bed.

"It's an inflatable bed-chair," Sherry said cheerfully, sliding into the room ahead of him. "It's great for bolstering yourself up while confined to a bed. Because you don't want to lie flat all the—"

"I'm not confined to a bed," he grated out. "I am not an invalid."

She plucked the offending object off the bed and shoved it aside. "I like to use it when I sit up reading at night," she said, still cheerful despite his rebuff. "Now then, where do you keep your pajamas?"

She started opening and closing the dresser drawers as if she had the perfect right.

"I don't wear pajamas."

"Oh. All right, then." She pulled the covers back on his double bed. "Sit down, and I'll help you—"

"Damn it, woman," he roared, "can't you see I don't want any help?"

She stared at him a moment, then looked down at the floor. "Yes," she said softly, "that's been obvious since I got here. It's also obvious to me that whether you want it or not you need some assistance."

"In case I haven't made myself clear yet, let me try again. You are to confine yourself to cooking, cleaning and caring for my children. I can take care of myself."

She picked up the bed-chair and pulled its plug. It made an awful noise as she squeezed the air out of it. "If that's what you wish." She didn't seem perturbed at all. "I'm only here to make things easier. If you need anything, call."

Jonathan could still smell her perfume after she left. Damn. He hadn't meant to be so rude. He knew she was only trying to do the job she'd been hired for. But the sight of her in his bedroom had made him snap. Having a woman like her anywhere near his bed was asking for trouble.

Besides, if she'd helped him undress, she'd have discovered exactly the effect she had on him. It would be highly embarrassing for Sherry to know she could turn him on just by walking across the room.

He allowed himself a brief fantasy—Sherry undressing him, cool, detached, her elegant hands touching him with a nurse's practical manner, those long nails lightly raking his skin. He let out an involuntary groan and hoped everyone in the house hadn't heard.

"I'M SORRY JONATHAN'S being such a bear," Allison said as she helped Sherry in the kitchen. "He's normally very nice, just reserved. But he's not used to being so helpless."

"Can you blame him, after I just about poisoned the whole family?"

"It was an honest mistake."

"Well, I'll remember from now on. No spicy food for the Hardisons." Sherry smiled, trying to get over the humiliation of ruining her very first meal here. "Listen, I know how some men are when they're injured. They feel weak, powerless, and they compensate by bullying everybody that crosses their paths. I'm used to it. It doesn't bother me." Although it did, a little. It was always important to her to do a good job, but she also wanted her patients to like her. Jonathan, she suspected, couldn't stand the sight of her.

Well, she'd always enjoyed a challenge.

"Maybe when the rest of us go, he'll simmer down some," Allison said.

"You're leaving now?" Sherry knew his whole family wouldn't be spending the night, but she was a little nervous about assuming full responsibility, especially for the children.

"Pete will be here one more night, but he and Sally are getting married tomorrow morning and taking off on their cruise."

"Does Jonathan expect to attend the wedding?" Sherry asked, concerned.

"He'd like to, but Jeff said no way."

"What about the children?"

"Yes. Pete will take them to the church, but if you could get them ready, that would be a big help."

"Okay." Sherry thought for a moment. "Where's the reception?"

"We're just having punch and cake at the church hall. It'll be a very small wedding. Why?"

"I don't mean to interfere, but I was just thinking, what if they moved the reception here? Then we could include Jonathan in the celebration."

Allison's eyes lit up. "That's a terrific idea! Let's run it past Pete and Sally and see what they think."

The older couple was enthusiastic about the suggestion. "I don't know why I didn't think of it myself," Sally said. "We haven't invited that many guests, so space isn't an issue, and I've always thought that church hall was ugly, anyway. I'll just call Gussie and Reenie and tell them to bring the refreshments and decorations here. Are you sure you don't mind?"

"Who, me?" Sherry laughed. "I *love* a party, any kind of party." She couldn't wait to tell Jonathan the good news—if he didn't throw something at her first.

JONATHAN WAS rudely awakened the next morning by a blast of sunlight. He opened his bleary eyes to find Sherry in his room, whisking curtains open.

"Good morning." *Whisk!* Another curtain open. But the bright sun could hardly compete with the woman herself. Wearing black leggings and a hot-pink, clingy shirt, her outrageous mountain of blond curls piled carelessly atop her head, she was an erotic fantasy come to life.

"Would you like breakfast in bed?" she asked cheerfully. "Or would you like to bathe and dress first and sit in your chair?"

He was aghast at her audacity. "You...you can't just barge in here without knocking!" he sputtered. "This isn't a hospital, it's my home, and *my* room."

He expected her to murmur an apology and slink away. But she didn't. He was quickly learning to expect the unexpected where his nursemaid was concerned.

"I did knock. You didn't answer. I had to check on you. Once I saw you were breathing—"

"You should have just left me in peace!"

"But it's late and you need to get up."

"Why, in God's name? Do I have an appointment with the President?"

She smiled, as if she had a secret. "You have a wedding reception to attend."

"Are you crazy? I can't go to Pete's wedding."

"You don't have to. The wedding's coming to you. Or at least, part of it. Pete and Sally have relocated the reception here, so you don't have to miss out on everything."

Jonathan couldn't believe what he was hearing. "All those people are coming *here?*" Great, just what he needed, for the whole town to witness his infirmity. "Forget it. It's not happening."

"You're not pleased?"

"I'm in no shape to entertain!"

"You won't have to lift a finger, I promise."

He sighed. The woman hadn't been here twenty-four hours and already she was driving him mad. He'd told Pete he regretted missing the wedding, but in reality, weddings weren't his cup of tea. They only served to remind him that his own marriage had been a dismal failure. All that lovey-dovey, till-death-do-us-part stuff made his divorced status that much more noticeable.

"Fine," he said through clenched teeth, since she seemed to be waiting for a decision from him. "I'll get dressed first, then have breakfast."

She beamed. "Great. I'll get your bathwater. Do you have a plastic tub somewhere I can use?"

"A plastic—" Suddenly he realized her intentions. "Oh, no, you don't. You and your sponge just keep away from me. I can manage on my own, thank you very much."

"Jonathan. You're in a full-leg cast. You can't take a regular bath or shower. Now, you don't have to be embarrassed. I've given hundreds of sponge baths—"

"No. If you're dying to bathe someone, bathe the kids. That ought to be enough challenge for you."

"They've already had their baths."

"Really?" He was impressed. Kristin didn't fight it too hard, if she had plenty of bubbles. But it took an act of Congress to get Sam in the tub.

"Well, Pete helped," she admitted.

He softened a bit toward Sherry. "Why don't you run along and see about breakfast? I'll be there shortly."

She shrugged. "All right. But before I go, I need to check you over."

Her words had a profound effect on him—unintended, he was sure. "What's to check?" he said gruffly. "The leg's in a cast."

But he saw by her implacable expression that she wouldn't take no for an answer. This was one fight he wasn't going to win. Jeff and Ed had both warned him about the complications that could arise from his injuries, especially his concussion. With a sigh, he allowed her to shine a flashlight in his face to see if his pupils would contract appropriately. She pointed a finger into the air and made him follow it with his eyes.

When she tried to pull the blankets off his cast he resisted—he was otherwise naked. But he finally relented and she was careful to keep the rest of his body modestly covered.

He lay back, closed his eyes and tried not to think about her touching him. She was gentler than any of the nurses at the hospital had been. She checked his toes for swelling and signs of poor circulation. Then she took his temperature to be sure he wasn't running a fever. He actually found himself enjoying Sherry's ministrations.

"All done."

He opened his eyes. She had that brilliant smile on her face again.

"You enjoy your work?" he asked.

"Oh, yes. Yes, I really do. And if there's anything I can do better, please tell me."

"There's just one thing."

"What?" She blinked her big green eyes at him, eyes that were enhanced with soft brown shadow, dark eyeliner and lashes that were so long and curly they should have been outlawed.

"Do you have to be so relentlessly cheerful?"

The smile drooped. "I'll try to adopt a more depressing attitude." And she left.

Jonathan immediately felt guilty, and well he should. What was it about this woman that brought out the absolute worst in him?

Chapter Three

Sherry knocked on Pete's bedroom door. "Pete? Is there anything I can do to help?"

Jonathan's grandfather opened the door, his hair sticking out wildly, his eyes reflecting blind panic. "I don't have any shoes! I bought a new suit for the weddin', but I forgot about dress shoes!"

"You must have something that would work."

"All I have is boots. Cowboy boots and work boots, one pair of Hush Puppies and house slippers."

"Let's see the boots."

When Pete showed her into his closet, she saw the problem. All of his boots were brown and his suit was blue. She selected the best-looking pair, brown ostrich skin. "I think I can make these work."

Pete looked doubtful. "If you say so."

She patted him on the arm. "I'll take care of it."

"Are the kids getting dressed?"

"I laid out their clothes."

"It'll take more than that."

Sherry checked her watch. She still had forty-five minutes before Pete and the kids had to leave for the church. "Sam! Kristin?" No answer. When she checked their rooms, their church clothes were untouched. Those rascals, they were probably hiding, testing her authority over them. She would have to be more stern, she knew. Soon Pete wouldn't be here to help her manage them.

She'd seen some black shoe polish under the sink. She gave the boots a makeover, then buffed them, bringing the ostrich skin to a shiny black finish. A rancher *should* get married in cowboy boots, she thought with a grin. She set them on newspaper to dry, then went in search of Jonathan's children. His breakfast would have to wait.

They weren't in the house. She stepped outside and called, but no answer. Slightly worried now, she ventured farther from the house, calling their names. "Come on, kids, you have to get dressed for Grandpa Pete's wedding!"

When they still didn't answer, she headed for the barn, the most logical place for them to be. When she stepped inside the modern building, she heard childish laughter and sighed with relief. "Kids? Children? Come on, now, it's time to get dressed for the—" She skidded to a stop when she spotted the children in an empty stall. They both leaned over a huge aquarium that sat on an old picnic table.

And they both did a really good job of ignoring her.

She came closer. "Do I need to clean the wax out of your ears? You don't want to be late for the wedding, do you?"

Sam finally looked up. "These are our pets, Alexander the Great and Miss Pooh. Here, see?" He reached into the aquarium, picked up something large and before she could react, plopped it on Sherry's shoulder.

She got a fleeting impression of slimy skin and huge, bulbous eyes, a cold, wet foot, or tentacle, or something touching her neck.

She screamed. The *thing,* whatever it was, leaped from her shoulder and landed on a hay bale.

"Get him!" Sam shouted. And both children dived for the creature, which Sherry could now see was an enormous bullfrog.

"No, you'll get dirty!" Sherry objected, ineffectually as it turned out. Both children were crawling around on the filthy stall floor, chasing after the slippery frog.

Finally they corralled the animal and returned it to its habitat. Only then did they turn their attention to Sherry, who was trembling with anger.

If they'd been about to giggle at her reaction to the frog, they stopped when they saw her face.

"Go back up to the house this instant," she ordered. "Wash your faces and hands, put on your church clothes, then sit in the living room, and *don't move* until it's time to leave for the wedding."

Sam gulped. "Yes, ma'am." He scurried away, followed by Kristin, who'd looked as if she were ready to cry.

Great. Jonathan hated her guts and now she'd made enemies of the children. At least Pete liked her.

Or so she thought.

Pete stood in the kitchen, bow tie in hand, staring

down at the black boots. "What in tarnation did you do to my ostrich boots?"

"I polished them."

"You turned them black! Missy, those are seven-hundred-dollar custom-made boots!"

"I don't understand. Can't boots be black?"

"But these are supposed to be brown!"

She was at a loss. She'd thought the boots looked much better after her polish job.

Just then, Jonathan hobbled into the kitchen. He wore the same pair of jeans as yesterday, one leg split up the center seam to accommodate his cast, but he'd also put on a starched dress shirt. He'd shaved and combed his wavy brown hair.

Her breathing came in shallow gasps.

"Problem?" he asked.

Sam and Kristin came running up to him, still dirty, still not dressed in the proper clothes. "Dad, Dad, Sherry yelled at us."

Jonathan spared a flickering gaze toward Sherry.

"They threw a frog at me," she said in her own defense. "And they weren't obeying me very well. I'm sorry I lost my temper, but I didn't want them to make Pete late for his own wedding." While she made this speech, she pulled a chair out for Jonathan to sit at the kitchen table. Though he'd said nothing, she could tell by the tension in his face that it hurt him to stand.

Jonathan sat down, then looked at his children. "Go wash up. And put on your church clothes," he said so quietly she almost didn't hear him.

They scrambled to do his bidding.

"See? No need to yell."

Right. She'd told the children exactly the same thing, but they hadn't listened to her. Were people like Jonathan born with a natural authority that children responded to? And had she been born without it? Or did it have something to do with her lack of parenting role models in her formative years?

If she ever wanted to have children of her own, she'd better figure that out.

Pete picked up his boots and, grumbling all the way, left the kitchen.

Jonathan watched him go, seeming faintly amused. Then he turned his gaze on Sherry. "Well, seems you're winning friends and influencing people this morning. If you can manage to burn my breakfast, you'll be four for four."

JONATHAN ACTUALLY FELT a bit sorry for Sherry as he watched her bustle around the kitchen, frying his eggs and toasting an English muffin. She was trying, he'd give her that. She might be a skilled nurse, but she obviously wasn't going to fit in here. He should have listened to Jeff.

He'd wait until after the wedding reception, he decided, then he would let her go.

With that decision made, Jonathan felt much more mellow. He went easier on Sherry, thanking her for breakfast and telling her it was good, even though she'd made his eggs too runny and the muffin too dark. No need to correct her. This was the last breakfast she would cook for him.

Pete and the kids got off to the wedding without

further incident. Sherry stood at the front door and waved to them. "Bye, good luck, Pete." Then the real fun began. Sally's two best friends, Gussie and Reenie, arrived with flowers and garlands, a wedding cake in the shape of a cowboy hat and enough food to feed a third-world country.

Sherry was obviously in her element. Gussie and Reenie, who thought of themselves as Cottonwood's social directors, were a little suspicious of her at first. From the recliner in the living room, where he pretended to read, Jonathan could see the two septuagenarians whispering to each other whenever Sherry stepped out of the room and shaking their heads disapprovingly.

But Sherry worked tirelessly, ironing a small wrinkle out of a tablecloth, rifling through cabinet after cabinet to find a punchbowl, quickly polishing a silver candelabra, pinching a brown leaf off a flower arrangement. She did whatever the two older women requested of her with a smile, complimented Gussie's horrific hat and even asked for Reenie's crab salad recipe.

Pretty soon the three women worked as a team, chattering and laughing as if they'd known each other for years.

Sherry did have a way about her, Jonathan conceded. She could drive him crazy in thirty seconds, but anyone could see she meant well. She didn't seem to have a malicious bone in her body.

Her very sexy body.

The way she was dressed, Jonathan couldn't help but notice her physical assets. She'd changed out of her earlier outfit and into a white, ruffly blouse that showed two inches of cleavage, paired with a red miniskirt and a wide black belt that made her waist look minuscule. Her legs were encased in black stockings, her feet in black spike heels with red polka-dots. She even had a red polka-dot bow in her hair, which cascaded around her shoulders and down her back in a waterfall of blond curls.

Her lips and fingernails, of course, were bright red, too.

When Sherry leaned down to pick up a runaway olive, she very nearly showed him her panties. Were they color-coordinated, too? Determinedly he buried his face in his book. It was useless to entertain fantasies about Sherry. Even if she wasn't going to be out of his life soon, she wasn't the type of woman he wanted to involve himself with. If he'd learned one thing from his marriage, it was that what turned him on wasn't what he needed to be happy.

Did that mean there was a type he *would* become involved with?

Good question. After his divorce from Rita, he swore he was done with women for good. But he supposed that was a pretty normal reaction. He didn't hate women. His brothers had managed to catch a couple of good ones. In fact, he'd been on a date not too long ago with Allison. He'd done it strictly to make Jeff jealous, but he'd found her company more pleasurable than he'd expected and that night he realized he missed female companionship.

But if he were to start dating again, he wouldn't date someone like Sherry. He would look for a country girl with simple tastes, one who understood and loved ranch life. Judging from the few comments she'd made, Sherry didn't know a steer from a bull. He would look for a woman who was good with children. Hard as she tried, Jonathan suspected Sherry had zero maternal instincts. His children were usually pretty easy to get along with, yet she'd managed to upset them somehow.

He would look for a woman who wasn't ashamed to buy clothes at Wal-Mart, one who didn't agonize over breaking a fingernail, one who didn't crave champagne and five-star dining experiences on a daily basis. The casual comment Sherry had made about credit card bills was a red flag. She was probably a shopaholic, like Rita.

Not that he minded an occasional shopping trip in Dallas or a special dinner out at a fancy steak-house. He wasn't cheap, and before his marriage he'd actually enjoyed treating a woman to special things now and then.

But Rita had wanted those treats in her life every day. She'd thought nothing of spending two hundred dollars on a pair of pants and then never wearing them. It wasn't that he couldn't afford her, the ranch made good money, but their priorities simply hadn't meshed.

When she'd suggested they hire a full-time nanny for the children, Jonathan had flatly refused. There was no practical need for professional child care. Rita didn't work outside the home and Pete would watch the kids virtually any time Rita asked. But all of her

Dallas and New Orleans friends had nannies, so she wanted to keep up.

She'd left him soon after that argument.

Jonathan sneaked another look at Sherry. High maintenance, that one. *Don't even think about it.*

Then, there wasn't time to think about anything because the wedding guests started to arrive—hundreds of them, or so it seemed. Each and every one of them had to pay his respects to Jonathan and ask all about the accident. He repeated the story so many times it became rote. Then people kept bringing him plates of food, precious little stuffed mushrooms, tiny quiches and pimento-cheese minisandwiches. He would have preferred some real food, like a roast beef sandwich. But his hired nurse was too busy playing hostess to see to his needs.

"You look like you swallowed an olive pit." This comment came from Jonathan's father. Edward perched on the arm of his recliner. "Is all this matrimonial bliss getting to you? First Wade and now Pete. In December it'll be Jeff and Allison."

That was as good an excuse as any. "Yeah, looks like you and me are the last hold-outs. You ever think about finding a woman?"

Edward laughed. "Me? Too set in my ways."

"That's what Pete used to say."

Edward sobered. "I couldn't do it. I just couldn't. Every woman I meet, I compare her to your mother and find her lacking."

"Mom was special, all right."

"You're not thinking of—"

"No, not me. All the good women in Cottonwood have been taken."

"Is that why we've started importing new ones?" Edward's gaze followed Sherry as she bustled around the room with a bottle of champagne in one hand and a plate of hors d'oeuvres in the other, refilling glasses and making sure everyone had everything they needed.

"No exotic imports for me," Jonathan said with an exaggerated shiver of revulsion. "Been there, done that."

By the time Pete and Sally had left for their honeymoon and the last guest had finally departed, Jonathan felt exhausted. He couldn't imagine why. All he'd done was sit in this blasted chair. He supposed small talk required more of an effort from him than most people. Being pleasant to casual acquaintances sapped his energy. He'd much rather spend time with his horses and cows, which didn't require conversation.

Sherry moved around the room with a trash bag, scooping up paper napkins, plates and plastic champagne glasses. "Well, I'd say that was a success."

"You would?" He looked at the devastation the party had wrought on his house.

"Oh, don't worry about the mess. I'll clean it up in a jiffy." She kicked off her high heels and continued her efforts. "It was just so nice, getting to meet everybody. Now when I see them in town, I won't be a stranger. Of course, I'm not sure all of them liked me. Anne's mother, Deborah Chatsworth, I thought was going to flip her wig when I pulled a champagne cork out with my teeth.''

''Deborah Chatsworth is something of a snob and her husband is worse. They wanted Anne to marry Jeff, have a doctor in the family. Instead, she went for Wade, an itinerant rodeo cowboy. But once they realized Anne and Wade were really in love, they accepted him. They're okay once you get to know them.'' Jonathan didn't add that Sherry wouldn't get that chance. She'd be gone.

''And Reverend Crane, Allison's father,'' she said. ''I burned my hand on a hot plate and I sort of let out a little curse. He turned so red I thought I was going to have to perform CPR on the spot.''

''You burned your hand?''

She held out one elegant, pale hand toward him, showing him a red mark on the outside of her little finger. ''No big deal, but it hurt like hell—I mean, heck.'' She cast worried glances around, but the children were nowhere in the vicinity. ''Shoot, where are those kids? I hope they changed clothes before running down to the barn to play with their frogs.''

''I doubt they did.''

''They're not mad at me anymore.''

Jonathan already knew that. Once she'd told them they could have all the cake and punch they wanted, since it was a special occasion and all, she'd instantly become their friend. He thought a nurse should know better.

She stopped halfway to the kitchen. ''Jonathan, is there anything I can get for you? I've kind of ignored you these past few hours.''

Nice of you to notice. "I could use some lunch."

She looked shocked. "How could you be hungry? I saw all those adoring women bringing you plates of food."

"Finger food. Itty-bitty pastries. Not enough to keep a mouse alive."

"Gee, I'm so stuffed I won't eat for a—" She stopped. "Of course, I'm not you. What would you like? There's leftover Frito-chili pie—oh, no, of course you wouldn't want that, it almost poisoned you. I could make you a sandwich or soup."

He hoped never to see that Frito-chili pie again. "Is there any roast beef?"

"I think so. Anne and Allison stocked the fridge pretty thoroughly."

"A sandwich, then, please."

"Okay."

Moments later he heard her clattering around in the kitchen and he started feeling guilty. She had enough to do, cleaning up after the party. Then again, there wouldn't have been a party if she hadn't arranged it.

A short time later she set a tray in front of him— a sliced barbecued-beef sandwich and a bowl of thick potato soup. He wasn't sure how she'd managed this. The soup tasted homemade. Maybe Anne or Allison had brought over some dishes already cooked, along with the groceries.

"Is that all right?"

"Mmm, yes, it's fine."

She smiled, then resumed her cleaning efforts.

He couldn't wait to hear what Deborah Chatsworth would say on the subject of his nurse, not to mention

Reverend Crane. In fact, he was pretty sure everyone who'd met Sherry would have an opinion on the subject.

What a relief it would be to tell them, ''She's already gone. I fired her.''

''Those choir ladies from the church sure seem nice,'' Sherry said as she sprayed some furniture polish on the coffee table.

Jonathan didn't know to which ladies she referred, since he seldom noticed the choir when he went to church. ''Mmm-hmm.''

''It's a shame, them missing out on their practice.''

''Mmm-hmm. What?''

''It seems Reverend Crane rented out the church hall to the high school dance squad to practice their routines while the gymnasium floor is being repaired. The church needs the money, so the choir ladies don't blame the reverend.''

''No, I don't imagine so.'' Jonathan picked up his book, hoping to discourage Sherry's idle chitchat. He wasn't much for flapping his gums just to fill silence. He soon learned, however, that this conversation had a very specific purpose.

''But the choir has no place to practice.''

''Can't they practice in the church?''

''Thin walls. They tried it once, but pretty soon they were all singing the disco song the dance squad was playing, and the dance squad girls were all kicking each other in the head because the singing next door was throwing off their rhythm.''

''That's a shame,'' he said.

''The reason I'm telling you all this is, well, I felt

sorry for them, so I invited them to come practice here.''

"What?" He couldn't have heard right.

"The invitation popped out of my mouth before I could stop it. There's plenty of space, if we move the furniture out of these two rooms." She indicated the living and dining rooms, which were separated only by a short bookcase. "And set out folding chairs—"

"Are you out of your mind?" he roared. "The church choir? Here?"

"The music will cheer you up. Doctors have done studies, you know, and—"

"The music will not cheer me up. Having fifty strange women in my house will make me exceedingly cranky."

"There are only thirty-two members in the choir."

"Look, Sherry. I don't like parties. I don't like company. And I particularly don't like a lot of jabbering women who only stop jabbering when they sing—off-key, I might add."

She looked stricken. "But I've already invited them."

"Then you can just uninvite them."

"But that would be rude."

"Did it ever occur to you that inviting them without consulting me first was rude? And this wedding reception—you didn't ask me about that, either. You just bulldozed ahead, like you owned the place."

"But I thought…I thought you'd be pleased. Allison mentioned how disappointed you were to miss the wedding, and I thought—"

"You thought wrong."

She drooped. "All right. I'll uninvite the choir. And next time I'll ask before I issue any invitations like that."

"There won't be a next time." Jonathan already felt like he'd kicked a puppy. He might as well get the rest of this over with.

Sherry blinked her green eyes at him a couple of times. "What?"

"Look, this isn't working out. You simply don't fit in here. It's obvious you can't manage the children. Yelling at them and then bribing them with sweets is no way to deal with kids. Anyway, I can take care of things myself. I've been getting around on the crutches okay."

Sherry faced him squarely, her hands on her slim hips. "You turn white as Wonder Bread every time you stand up and totter around on those crutches. You most certainly cannot take care of yourself. How are you going to look after those kids? They move faster than the speed of light."

"I'll manage."

"How will you cook for them?"

"That's what a microwave is for. It couldn't be any worse than—" He stopped himself, but she already knew what he was going to say.

"I got the message. You hate my cooking."

"It's a bit spicy. We're used to more basic fare. Don't worry, I'll pay you for the time you've been here, plus a few days extra for the trouble you went to."

"I can do better. All you have to do is tell me when you don't like something, and I'll..." her voice trailed off when she realized Jonathan wasn't going to budge. She slumped in defeat. "All right, then. I'll just finish cleaning up in here, then I'll pack my things."

"Leave the mess. I have a service that comes every two weeks. They'll be here Monday morning."

She slowly set down the plastic cup she'd been holding. She stared at him a moment, eyes challenging, but only for a moment. Then she swept from the room.

He'd made her cry, he realized. He hadn't intended to be harsh. He just wanted her gone. Surely even she could see that this wasn't a compatible employer-employee relationship.

Chapter Four

Sherry waited until she reached the safety of her room before she let the tears fly. How could she have read the situation so wrong? She'd thought everything was going pretty well. She'd thought having the wedding reception here was a stroke of genius. She'd thought inviting the choir to sing here would cheer Jonathan up. Lord knew his mood needed improvement.

But she'd been completely off the mark.

What was wrong with her? Jonathan's words echoed in her head as she hastily packed her clothes. *You don't fit in here.* That was what the office manager at her last job had said when she'd fired Sherry. *Too flamboyant. Too colorful. Too loud for a prestigious medical practice.* Later, she'd overheard one of the other nurses describe Sherry, using the word "cheap."

Though the criticisms had hurt, Sherry had eventually been able to dismiss them. Dr. Crossly's office was a snobbish operation where patients felt privileged to be overcharged, and the nurses were valued for their family connections over their medical skills. She'd even convinced herself that those drab nurses she worked with had been jealous of her natural charm and had conspired to get rid of her.

Now she was beginning to wonder if there wasn't a grain of truth in the criticisms. Was her trailer-trash upbringing so apparent? She liked to think of herself as stylish. She pored over fashion magazines, then haunted discount stores and designer outlets, recreating the outfits, following the dos and don'ts. Maybe her personal style wasn't just a bit colorful, but loud and trashy?

What would she have to look like to "fit in" in Jonathan's world? Thinking back to the wedding guests, she recalled several who'd worn bright colors and high heels. Some had even worn hats. So it wasn't her clothes that set her apart.

If it wasn't her clothes, it must be her behavior. Did she laugh too loud? Talk too much?

Oh, well, what did it matter? She was leaving Cottonwood and she'd probably never set foot within the town limits again.

Sherry changed out of her dress-up clothes and into comfortable leggings and a long sweater for the drive home. When everything else was packed, she started hauling her bags to the front door. Jonathan, still ensconced in his chair, hid behind his book and pretended he didn't see her.

She was on her third trip when Sam entered the living room. "Dad? Kristin has a stomachache."

"I'm not surprised," Jonathan said in a grumpy voice. "She must have eaten four pieces of cake and I don't know how much punch she drank."

"She says it really hurts."

"Get her some Pepto-Bismol. It's in the medicine chest in my bathroom."

"I'll check on her," Sherry said automatically.

Jonathan gave her a dark look. "I think you've done enough."

Sherry ignored him and headed for Kristin's bedroom. Fired or not, she wasn't going to ignore a child in pain, especially if it was her fault.

When she entered Kristin's room, the sight that greeted her was disturbing to say the least. Kristin lay on the bed, still in her fancy dress, holding her stomach and moaning softly.

Sherry sat on the edge of her bed. "Kristin?"

"It hurts," Kristin said, almost in tears.

"I'm going to do what I can to make it better, okay?" She felt the little girl's forehead. It was hot to the touch. She turned to Sam, who was watching anxiously. "Sam, can you get me a thermometer?"

He nodded and bolted out of the room to do her bidding.

Sherry gently palpated Kristin's stomach and abdomen, and almost immediately found the source of the pain. The child had a hot appendix, Sherry would stake her life on it. She'd seen dozens of similar cases when she'd worked in emergency medicine.

"Hate to tell you, punkin', but you're going to the hospital."

Kristin started crying in earnest. "I *hate* the hospital. All they do is stick you with needles."

"I know, sweetie, but they only do it so you can get well." Pushed by adrenaline, Sherry lifted Kristin into her arms and carried her to the living room.

Jonathan, thank God, grasped the urgency of the situation immediately. "What's wrong with her?"

"Her appendix. I'm taking her to the hospital. Where's the closest one?"

"Tyler. Out Highway 60, north. When you reach Tyler, turn left at the first light. Hospital's about half a mile on the right."

Sherry listened as she grabbed her purse and her keys, somehow juggling everything and Kristin, too. "Got it. Call ahead and let them know I'm coming. Tell them it's urgent."

"Okay. Jeff or my dad will meet you there."

"Right. Sam, you stay here and take care of your dad."

Sam, whose face had gone white, nodded.

Less than a minute later, Sherry strapped Kristin into the passenger seat of the Firebird, hit the gas and zoomed down the driveway. She could have called an ambulance, but she'd been afraid that out in the country medical help would take too long to arrive. She, on the other hand, had a fast car and the nerve to give it the gas.

"You've been to the hospital before?" Sherry asked Kristin, hoping to distract her from the pain.

She nodded miserably. "Cut my head—had to have an operation."

"Oh, that doesn't sound like much fun. How did it happen?"

"I was jumping on the bed…fell off."

Sherry had seen her share of those types of accidents. In fact, she'd been one of them. The infamous bike accident. Except she hadn't been riding a bike.

Her father had broken a chair over her head when as a teenager she'd told him she was pregnant. But now wasn't the time to dwell on her past mistakes or the child she'd given up. She had a child in the here and now who needed her full attention.

Sherry had no trouble finding the hospital. When she pulled into emergency, two orderlies and a gurney were there to meet them. The orderlies took Kristin from the car, strapped her onto the gurney and whisked her inside just as Jeff's Porsche pulled up.

He jumped out, leaving the engine running and ran up to Sherry. "What happened?"

"Stomachache, nausea, high fever, extreme sensitivity in the lower right abdomen."

"Could be a lot of—"

"It's her appendix."

"No offense, Sherry, but you're not a—"

"I'm a nurse practitioner and I'm qualified to make a diagnosis. It's her appendix." She turned and headed back to her car.

"Wait, where are you going?"

"Back to Dallas. Your brick-headed brother fired me, and by law that means I have to leave."

Though she wanted to stay until Kristin was out of danger, she couldn't. She had no right. She'd gotten Kristin into competent medical hands, and that meant her role in the Hardison family was over. She climbed back into her car and took off, before Jeff could see she was crying…again.

SAM HAD LONG AGO stopped wanting to be cuddled, but this night he crawled into Jonathan's recliner with him, somehow managing to avoid jostling the broken leg.

"Is Kristy gonna be all right?"

"We'll know more soon," Jonathan said.

"How come she's always going to the hospital? I never went, not once."

Jonathan shook his head ruefully. "Seems there's one in every family. When we were kids, it was your uncle Wade who was always getting into trouble—falling off horses, mostly, but sometimes other things. He fell in a bed of fire ants once and had such a bad reaction he had to go to the emergency room." Now Jonathan knew what their parents had gone through. At least when Kristin had been injured last year, Jonathan had been able to go to the hospital and be with her. Now he was relegated to waiting at home for the phone to ring.

"Dad? Was Sherry leaving?"

"Um, yeah."

"Why? Didn't she like us? I 'pologized for putting the frog on her."

"No, she liked us. It's my fault. I fired her."

Sam's clear eyes clouded with confusion. "Why would you do that?"

"I thought we didn't need her."

"But, Dad, if she hadn't been here—"

"I know, I know." He sighed. "She probably saved Kristin's life."

"Then she can stay?"

"I'm not sure she'll want to stay now," Jonathan admitted. "I think I hurt her feelings."

"Then just 'pologize. That's what you're always

telling me to do when I do something wrong. Besides, she'll stay if she knows we need her.''

Jonathan was amazed his eight-year-old was so perceptive. In a very short time, he'd figured out what drove Sherry. She needed to be needed.

Hell, if she wanted need, he'd give her need, and he'd give her a damn apology, too.

Two hours after Sherry had left with Kristin, the phone rang, and Jeff was on the other end of the line. "Kristin's fine," he said without preamble. "Sherry was right, it was her appendix. They rushed her to surgery and took it out, probably minutes before it would have ruptured. But she came through the surgery just fine. They'll want to keep her here a couple of days.''

Jonathan's stomach roiled with a mixture of relief and guilt. "My God," he muttered, "and I wanted to give her Pepto-Bismol.''

"It's a good thing Sherry was there. Yeah, she's a gem, all right.''

Jonathan recognized the goading tone in Jeff's voice. "I suppose she told you I fired her.''

"What did you go and do that for?''

Jonathan covered the mouthpiece. "Sam, take Sherry's luggage and put it back in her room.''

"Yay! She's staying!" Sam clambered off the recliner and started hauling suitcases toward the back of the house.

"Jonathan?" Jeff said. "You there?''

"I was either going to fire her or take her to bed," Jonathan admitted in a hoarse whisper, truthful with himself for the first time. "I didn't think the latter was a viable option."

Jeff just laughed. "You're kidding, right?"

"I wish I were."

"So take her to bed. What's the big deal?"

"Even if she were so inclined—which she's not, now that I've alienated her—I would not be sleeping with the nurse while the children are around."

"I'll treat them to a movie," Jeff said, laughing. "Maybe a double feature."

"You're not taking this very seriously. It's far too complicated. I can't sleep with Sherry. I'm not like you, like you used to be. I can't just sleep with a woman and then discard her."

To his credit Jeff did stop laughing. "I guess anything more serious than a one-night stand is out of the question?"

"Of course it is. You're the one who so strenuously opposed bringing Sherry to Cottonwood in the first place. Now you think she ought to be my girlfriend?"

"It's just that I wouldn't rule anything out. Granted, she can't cook and she scandalized half the people at Pete and Sally's wedding reception, but she charmed the other half silly. Even I'll admit she has her...strong points."

Jon was so frustrated with the conversation that he hung up. He never should have said anything to Jeff because now he'd probably never hear the end of it. But then he realized he wanted more news about Kristin, so he called Jeff's cell number and hounded him for details.

Sherry showed up a few minutes later. Jonathan,

who'd managed to pull himself out of the recliner with Sam's help, was hiding in his room, rehearsing what he was going to say to her. He heard her come in the front door.

"Jon? Jonathan? Hey, where is everybody? What happened to my stuff?"

Sam ran from his room down the hall and into the living room, quick as a bullet. "Hi, Sherry, guess what! Dad says you can stay!" he said all in one breath.

"Oh, really?"

This was bad, Jonathan thought, listening to the exchange. She'd had a little time to think over his rudeness, he realized, and she no longer wanted to stay. He was going to have to do some fancy back-pedaling. He hoisted himself onto the crutches and made his laborious way toward the living room.

"You're gonna stay now, aren't you?" Sam asked. "Whatever Dad said, he didn't mean it. He's extra cranky on account of his leg being broke and all."

That was an understatement. Jonathan limped into the room. He caught Sherry's gaze. She stared at him hard, until he was forced to look away.

"Sam," he said as he sat down on the sofa, "could you—"

"Yeah, I know. Grown-up stuff. Don't forget to tell her about Kristin, Dad." And he bounded out of the room.

"Is she going to be all right?" Sherry asked.

Jonathan nodded. "Had her appendix out. Jeff says she's doing well, thanks to you."

Sherry shook her head, her blond curls flying in

every direction. "You would have realized in another moment or two that something was wrong. You'd have called an ambulance and everything would have been fine."

"If you don't want to take credit for saving my daughter's life, I'll understand. It's a big responsibility."

"I'd just as soon you didn't make a big deal of it."

She was serious. He wondered what that was about. "I had Sam put your bags back in your room."

"Then he can just help me take them out again. I'm not staying where I'm not wanted."

"You are wanted. More than that, you're needed. You're right, I can't take care of the kids by myself, especially now that Kristin's going to be recuperating, too. I'd feel much more comfortable if you were here to keep an eye on her. On all of us."

She eyed him skeptically. "You're sure you're not doing this out of guilt or gratitude?"

"I'm sure."

She still didn't jump at the chance to stay.

"I'm sorry I was rude to you," he added for good measure. "Sam's right. I *am* cranky. Not that it's any excuse, but I haven't been sleeping."

Immediately a look of concern crossed her face. "If the pain is keeping you awake, you should take the medication that was prescribed. I noticed the pills I put out for you last night were still there this morning."

"I don't like taking pills. I've seen too many people get hooked on those things."

"Yeah, me, too. Tell you what, I'll give you one

tonight and one tomorrow night, just so you can sleep, then no more. I'll flush the rest.''

"Does that mean you'll be here tomorrow?''

Ah, he'd caught her. She looked away, embarrassed. "Okay, but I have one condition.''

"Name it.''

"Let the choir practice here.'' She pleaded with her eyes. "I just can't face calling Betty Bruno and telling her she and her ladies can't come here after all.''

Jonathan gritted his teeth. "All right, fine.'' Maybe by the time they got there, he would be well enough to work in his office in the barn for an hour or two.

She clapped her hands together. "All right, then. I didn't really want to lug all those bags out to the car. You'll help me to do things the way you like? I got it that you don't like spicy food and no more parties without your okay. What else?''

"I...I can't think of anything else offhand.''

"Oh, come on now. The children—no more yelling, no more bribes and not so many sweets. Now, in all honesty, I didn't really yell. I spoke firmly.''

Jonathan found himself grinning. "I'm sure you did.''

"What else? How else do I not fit in? If you could be more specific, I'd work on it.''

"Sherry, you're fine. Mother Teresa herself could have been my nurse and I probably would have complained. It just bruises my ego a bit that I *need* a nurse. I'll get over it.''

"Well, okay,'' she said dubiously. "If you think of anything, tell me. What would you and Sam like

for dinner? I make a mean macaroni and cheese casserole.''

"That sounds fine.'' If it was dreadful, he could
always raid the refrigerator after she'd gone to bed.

SHERRY PUT HER CLOTHES BACK in the closet, hum-
ming softly. She was way too happy about all this.
On the drive home from Tyler, she'd convinced herself that leaving the Hardison Ranch was the best
course of action. Being a live-in caregiver was a dicey
proposition, and if the chemistry wasn't right it wasn't
right. No reason to kick herself and assume all the
blame.

And their chemistry was all wrong.

Well, *wrong* didn't accurately describe it. More
like *explosive.* She felt hot and bothered whenever she
was within ten feet of the man. How could she be an
adequate nurse when she was so distracted?

But when Jonathan had given her a reprieve, she'd
offered only token resistance. She ought to have more
pride, she thought. He'd said some pretty mean things
to her.

She sighed. She'd never had it in her to hold a
grudge. Take Allison, for example. Sherry had wanted
to despise Allie for stealing Jeff away from her, but
she couldn't because Allison was really nice—and
Jeff hadn't actually been Sherry's to steal.

Sherry was even still friendly with her parents, despite the crummy childhood they'd treated her to. After she'd left home and refused to see them, their
marriage, never very strong to begin with, had dis-
integrated and they'd divorced. But they'd also both

quit drinking. Sober, they weren't really bad people. They'd apologized for the things they'd said and done when she was pregnant with Brandon, and they'd tried to make it up to her.

What more could they do? Nothing would bring her son back, so there was no use being bitter and vengeful toward her parents the rest of her life.

Dinner was only a mild success. She hadn't realized that the Hardison men expected meat with their macaroni and cheese. She supposed it made sense that people raised on a cattle ranch would grow accustomed to beef. She gently pointed out the health drawbacks of a steady diet of red meat, then sliced up the rest of the roast for them. Sam only picked at his salad—she'd put "too much stuff" in it. He didn't care for green onions and cucumbers. Jonathan ate some of his, but she noticed he carefully picked out the green peppers.

She added this new knowledge about her employers' eating habits to her mental storehouse.

"What's for dessert?" Sam asked.

Sherry got up and peeked into the freezer, relieved at what she saw there. "Ice cream?"

"And pie?" Sam asked hopefully.

Sherry was pretty sure there was no pie.

"We don't need pie every single night, Sam," Jonathan said diplomatically. He'd insisted on sitting at the table tonight, his leg propped up on a chair. "Ice cream is fine."

Later, Sherry took one pill from Jonathan's prescription bottle and filled a glass with water—filtered water from the pitcher in the fridge, not from the tap.

That was another thing she'd learned she'd been do-ing wrong. The well water from the tap tasted awful.

She knocked softly on Jonathan's door.

"Come in."

She found him in bed, leaning against the flowered bed-chair and reading a book. "You look comfort-able."

"This thing's pretty useful." He gave it a pat.

"I brought you the pain pill."

"I don't think I'll take it after all. I want to be alert in case the hospital calls."

Sherry sighed and left the pill and water on the night stand. "In case you change your mind. Can I get you anything else?"

"No. Sherry, you don't have to wait on me hand and foot. I'll holler if I need something."

"You won't, though. I can tell that leg is hurting you. You have a pinched look around your mouth. But you haven't complained once."

"It is twingeing a mite. I probably did too much today."

Twingeing. He must have a high pain threshold. She went into the bathroom, rummaged around in the cabinet until she found what she wanted, and tried not to notice Jonathan's personal things—soap, razor, af-tershave, macho stick antiperspirant.

Wordlessly she handed him the aspirin. He took them. She watched his Adam's apple bobbing up and down as he swallowed. Fascinating. Then she left, her body throbbing from her scalp to her toes, vowing she would stay out of his bedroom. He looked much too inviting, snuggled up under those blankets with *her* bed-chair.

Chapter Five

On Sunday, the next morning, Jeff came by to take Jonathan and Sam to the hospital to visit Kristin. Jonathan had insisted, though it was a pretty big production to get him out of the house and into a car. Jeff had agreed to the outing only when Jonathan promised to use a wheelchair at the hospital.

Left to her own devices, Sherry decided to clean. Jonathan had said to leave the mess from the wedding reception until Monday, but she couldn't do it. So she went to work. She figured she had plenty of nervous energy to burn off. Maintaining a professional demeanor around Jonathan was harder than she'd thought, when all her female instincts told her to flirt, flirt, flirt!

Not that it would do any good, she thought as she stuffed the last of the trash bags into a garbage can in the garage. He was immune to her. She suspected Jonathan Hardison would not fall for any of her usual lines, if she were inclined to use one, which she wasn't. Not while he was her patient and employer. But this gig wouldn't last forever....

The doorbell rang and Sherry rushed from the garage to see who was calling. She was pleased to see Allison standing on the front porch.

"Thought you might be lonesome," Allison said with a knowing smile as she swept in.

"'Lonesome' isn't exactly the word. You want some tea?"

"Sure."

They settled in the kitchen and talked while Sherry went through the familiar, comfortable motions of putting on the kettle and assembling the fixings for tea.

"I'm surprised you're still talking to me," Allison said.

"What? Why wouldn't I?"

"Because I got you into this. I've heard through the grapevine that Jonathan is behaving like a perfect beast and the children have been throwing frogs at you."

Sherry dismissed Allison's comment with a wave of her hand. "It's not them, it's me," she admitted. "I thought I was imminently qualified for a job like this, but it's much harder than I thought it would be. I'm not at all what Jonathan expected. Last night he fired me, you know."

"I heard. Beast," Allison muttered.

"He only relented because I recognized Kristin's symptoms for what they were and got her to the hospital. He's keeping me on out of gratitude and guilt."

"I don't understand. What have you done that Jonathan so disapproves of?"

"Well, let's see. I can't cook and I'm terrible with the children because I yell at them, then bribe them with sweets. I'm too cheerful. I invited people to the house without his prior approval.''

"Is any of that true?"

"Well, sort of. But Jonathan was fishing for excuses. I suspect the real reason he fired me was because he just doesn't like me. He says I don't fit in. I did manage to alienate a few people at the wedding reception—your father, for one, and Anne's mother.''

"Oh, please. The two most easily alienated people in town," Allison said with a smirk.

The kettle boiled and Sherry poured hot water into their teacups. "He may have a point," she said carefully. "This isn't the first time this problem has cropped up. I was fired from my last job for much the same nebulous reasons. My supervisor said I didn't fit in.'' She settled into her chair and idly fiddled with her teabag. "I'm beginning to think there *is* something wrong with me," she admitted.

"There's nothing wrong with you," Allison insisted. "You're an original. Unique. You don't look, act or talk like every other woman in the world, and I think that's refreshing.''

"I stand out. Is that what you're saying?"

"Well, yeah, I guess," Allison agreed.

"I used to think it was good to stand out in a crowd. But I'm beginning to think sometimes it's better to blend in, so people don't think you're loud and flamboyant and…and cheap.''

Allison gasped. "Did Jonathan say that?"

"No, but if he had, it wouldn't be the first time. Be honest, what did you think of me when we first met?'' She realized she was putting her friend on the spot. But this was something she needed to know.

''I thought you were glamorous and very friendly.'' Allison said, as she tried to hide behind her cup of tea.

''Tell me the truth, girlfriend.''

Allison set down her cup. ''All right, but you asked for it. You struck me as a woman on the prowl. Sexually confident, but a little too forward...a little obvious.''

''Obvious?'' That was a new one.

''Like you were advertising.''

''Like you weren't, Miss Miracle Bra?'' Sherry knew now that Allison had come to that medical products convention for the sole purpose of catching Jeff's attention and seducing him. She'd succeeded admirably.

''I was, you're right. But we're not talking about me.''

''But maybe we should. You dress in sexy clothes, but nobody calls you cheap and trashy.''

Allison was looking very uncomfortable.

''Please, you're my friend. *Tell* me. I just want to figure out what I'm doing wrong so I can fix it and then Jonathan won't hate me.''

''Okay. It's not just the clothes. It's the whole package. You have a style all your own, and it would be perfectly appropriate in some places—at a night club in Dallas, for example. But it tends to make you stand out in...professional situations. And in a place like Cottonwood.''

Sherry pulled a magnetic notepad off the refrigerator door and started taking notes. "So the clothes are part of it."

"Like those leather pants you're wearing. Gorgeous. Very stylish."

Sherry smiled. "You like them? Got them on closeout at Leather Wearhouse. Forty-two dollars."

"But they're out of place here. Then there's the makeup. You wear an awful lot of it. Fine for evening in a dark restaurant, not so good for broad daylight."

Sherry was quaking inside, but she took down everything Allison was saying. She'd asked, after all. "Okay, what else?"

"The two-inch fingernails."

Sherry inspected her nails. Then she popped one off. "They're just the press-on kind. If I don't wear them, I bite my nails." One of those childhood habits she never quite kicked.

"Fine, just make them shorter." Allison held out her own modest nails, coated with only clear polish.

"Okay."

"The spike heels have got to go. Don't you own any flats or sneakers?"

Sherry leaned under the table and inspected Allison's shoes. She was wearing flat-heeled boots.

"I'm paying a social call," Allison pointed out. "I'm not doing housework."

"I might have a pair of flat shoes somewhere," Sherry said glumly, making a note.

"And finally, the hair."

"What's wrong with my hair?" Sherry almost wailed. "It's my best feature."

"You have great hair. I'd kill to have it. But it's…"

"Go ahead," Sherry said, wincing. "I can take it."

"It's too big and it's too blond. I'm not saying you should shave it off, just downplay it a little."

"I'm not sure I know what you mean."

Allison took her cell phone out of her purse. "Let's call Anne. She's the world's best at makeovers. She turned me from a frump to a…well, whatever I am now. I bet she can help you."

"Oh, yes. Yes, call her. I want to be made over, or rather, made-under. Tell her I want to look and act like someone Jonathan would…approve of."

Allison paused. "Are you sure about this? I still think you're fine the way you are."

"Obviously I'm not. I need an overhaul. Call her. Now, just do it."

"YOU BROUGHT ALL THIS for two weeks?" Anne examined Sherry's wardrobe thoughtfully, sliding the coat hangers from left to right as she considered and then dismissed each garment.

"I wasn't sure what would be appropriate." Sherry caught a glance at herself in the dresser mirror and jumped. For the past couple of hours she'd been getting a crash course from Anne and Allison on how to dress like a woman Jonathan Hardison might like and respect.

Both women had been reluctant to overhaul Sherry too radically. "It's no good changing yourself to please other people," Anne had said. "You'll just end up feeling like a fake, an impostor, and you won't be happy with yourself."

"I haven't been really happy with myself for a while now," Sherry had argued. "C'mon, it's just an experiment. I'm thirty-one years old. Maybe it's time I looked a little more *Good Housekeeping,* and a little less *Cosmopolitan.*"

In the end Anne and Allison had agreed to the makeover. They'd cut six inches off Sherry's hair, relaxed the curls and toned down the blond. They'd scrubbed her face clean, then applied very small amounts of makeup in subdued colors. They'd exchanged her dangly earrings and multiple rings on her fingers for small gold hoops for her ears and one discreet opal ring on her right hand. They'd gotten rid of the press-on nails and polished her natural nails with clear polish. Now they were working on her clothes.

"Okay, this might work." Anne had selected a rather ordinary pair of jeans, a plain, peach-colored blouse and a pair of black canvas shoes.

"That's the kind of stuff I wear around the house when no one sees me," Sherry argued. "Can I at least jazz it up with my rhinestone belt?"

"No," Allison and Anne said together.

"And ditch the push-up bra," Anne added.

"I don't have any other kind. Well, except an athletic bra, but that's for aerobics."

"Wear the athletic bra," Anne said. "You don't exactly need help in that department."

Sherry looked down at her breasts. She'd been stacked since she was fourteen and she'd always been proud of her bustline. She had her doubts about down-playing one of her best features, but she'd put her trust into these women's hands.

"All right, I'll try."

After she'd changed her clothes and shoes, she examined herself in the mirror. She could have passed for a preacher's daughter. But it wasn't bad, she decided. Just different. And if changing her facade meant her patients, co-workers and other people in general would stop looking down on her, she was willing to try.

Oh, who was she kidding? The changes were for Jonathan. She wanted—needed—for him to like her. She knew darn well that seeking approval from men was one of her weaknesses, but it wasn't a habit she could easily toss aside.

"I really need to get home," Anne said. "I stuck Wade with Olivia when he needs to be getting ready for his Thanksgiving week camp session."

"Me, too," Allison said as she put on her jacket. "I haven't bicycled yet today."

Sherry thanked them profusely. Once they were gone, she got out the only cookbook she could find in the Hardison Ranch kitchen and tried to figure out how to bake a pie from scratch. She wanted to surprise Sam.

"Do you think we did the right thing?" Allison asked Anne as she drove down the lane toward Anne and Wade's place, which was on land adjacent to the ranch.

"She looked great when we were done," Anne

said. "There's nothing wrong with a makeover, as we both know from experience. Remember, you resisted me at first when I wanted to change everything about you."

That was true. Allison had been startled by the results of her makeover. She'd gone from a plain Jane to a femme fatale in two evenings. But she'd learned the hard way that outer trappings didn't make or break a relationship. She was afraid Sherry was still in that I-have-to-catch-a-man-before-I'm-too-old mode, and she was working on the outer stuff when she ought to be changing what was on the inside.

"Do you think she has the hots for Jonathan?" Anne asked.

"Yup, but she won't do anything about it while he's under her care. I'm pretty sure about that."

"But once the job is done…"

"Then all bets are off. She can be relentless, just ask Jeff."

"Jonathan could use someone like Sherry in his life," Anne said thoughtfully. "He needs to unbend a little. But he wasn't going to take her seriously the way she looked before. I think she reminded him too much of Rita."

"Eww, Sherry's nothing like Rita, thank God."

"Yeah, but they're both into clothes and makeup and jewelry. I think that's what Jon sees. If he could get past that, he might really like Sherry."

JONATHAN HAD STAYED way too long at the hospital and he was paying for it now. As Jeff drove him and Sam back to the ranch, Jonathan's leg throbbed and every muscle was sore from using the crutches because he'd refused the wheelchair even after he'd promised. But he hadn't been able to tear himself away from his little girl. He was so grateful she was all right and so guilty that his disinterest in her stomachache could have cost her her life.

"When you get home, you better take one of those pain pills I prescribed," Jeff said.

"Is it that obvious?"

"I can see it in the way you hold your mouth."

"Hmm. That's what Sherry said."

"She's a good nurse. She nailed Kristin's diagnosis. I was playing the arrogant doctor, assuming I knew better, but she was right."

Jonathan glanced over his shoulder at Sam, who was listening to his MP3 player with headphones. "Sherry might be a good nurse, but everything else about her drives me insane."

Jeff just laughed. "You always did go for the fancy-looking ones. I remember in high school, that cheerleader, what was her name?"

Jon groaned. "Lola."

"That's the one. You used to practically fall out of the bleachers every time she did the splits."

"Yeah, and what happened to her? She ran off to some city and became a stripper."

"With a name like that, what choice did she have? Let's see, then there was that girl—"

"There's no need to go over the list. We all know I have abysmal taste in women, ending with my ex-wife."

"Rita was pretty."

"Rita was gorgeous, and about the most useless woman in the world. It still surprises me that she has a career now. I guess she was just useless around me."

"Sherry's not useless."

"Don't start. It wouldn't work. She's just too...I don't know. Too flamboyant, I guess. I'm counting the days till Pete and Sally come back so I can send Sherry back to Dallas without feeling guilty."

Jeff just raised one eyebrow and said nothing. They were pulling up to the house.

"I can do this myself," Jonathan said when Jeff started to get out so he could help his brother to the door.

"No dice. I'm going in to make sure you take a pill."

"What is it with you medical people and pills? Sherry's been pushing me to take them, too."

"We're not trying to get you addicted. It's just that you'll heal faster if you're not stressed out with pain. Stop being so macho."

Sam ran ahead of the two men and opened the door. "Mmm, something smells good."

Sure enough, something did. "Sherry?" Jonathan called out.

"In the kitchen. Just a second." He heard some clattering around. Then, moments later, she appeared.

At least, he *thought* it was Sherry. He must have been gaping because she flashed an embarrassed grin. "It's me, all right. Allison and Anne dropped by and we did, you know, girl things—hair and makeup."

"You look great," Jeff said, for which Jonathan

was grateful, since he couldn't get any words past his lips. She looked nice, he supposed, but she didn't look like Sherry anymore. Gone was the cascade of bleached-blond curls that reached the middle of her back. Now her hair fell in gentle waves to just past her shoulders—and it was brown. Almost brown, anyway, with just a hint of gold highlights.

But the changes didn't stop there. What happened to those glossy red lips? Was she actually wearing lipstick at all? And those huge earrings that looked like chandeliers had been replaced with tiny gold loops. Her clothes could only be described as sedate, and her shoes had no heels whatsoever. Even her voice seemed more subdued.

With an inward groan, he realized this metamorphosis was his doing.

She rushed over to help Jonathan into his favorite recliner. This time he didn't resist her help. He was exhausted.

"Sit down before you fall down. Jeff, really, you shouldn't have kept him out so long."

"I couldn't drag him away from Kristin's bed."

Sherry's face softened. "How's she doing?"

"She's great," Jeff said. "And, Sherry, I want to apologize for what I said last night. I was being an arrogant jerk."

"Oh, I'm used to doctors being that way," she said, but it was clear she was teasing. "Seriously, don't give it another thought."

"Hey, is something burning?" Sam asked.

Sherry gasped. "My pie!" And she rushed toward the kitchen with Sam at her heels.

"What are you laughing about?" Jonathan said to his brother, who appeared highly amused by the whole turn of events.

"You can't claim she's too flamboyant now. I think even my future in-laws would approve of her."

"YOU CHANGED," Sam commented, as Sherry put the finishing touches on dinner.

"Women do that sometimes," she said breezily, though inside she was a jumble of insecurities. Did Jonathan like the new Sherry? He'd noticed right away, and she supposed that was good, but he hadn't said much. He'd been way too quiet, hiding behind his book. "We like to try out a new image sometimes, you know. It's fun."

"Why's it fun?"

She shrugged. "I don't know. Haven't you ever wanted to be someone else or at least look like someone else?"

Sam seemed to consider her question carefully. "Not really. Except maybe when I was a little kid and I wanted to be Spiderman, but that was dumb."

"I guess that's the difference between you and me," Sherry said. "You're happy with who you are. I'm still trying to figure out who I am." She filled a glass with ice cubes and tea, then set it on a tray with the rest of Jonathan's meal. "Here, you can take this to your dad." She'd insisted he stay put for dinner instead of coming to the table. He'd been upright long enough for one day.

As Sam carefully balanced the tray and carried it out of the kitchen, Sherry gave a rueful look to her cherry pie. It was probably edible, but one half of the crust was burned. Shoot, why couldn't she have done one thing right?

She and Sam ate their meals on TV trays in the living room, so Jonathan wouldn't have to eat alone. But he said almost nothing during the meal, just kept shooting her curious glances, as if she were some specimen of bug that he wanted to figure out.

"The choir's coming over tonight," she said as she picked up her tray.

Jonathan groaned.

"I was afraid you'd forgotten. Listen, you don't even have to talk to them if you don't want to. I can tell them you're resting."

"I fully intend to barricade myself in my room until they're gone," he said. "And if I can find a pair of earplugs, I'm wearing them." With that cheerful pronouncement, he levered himself out of the chair and hobbled out of the room.

"He's being grumpy again," Sam said apologetically.

"He's allowed. I think his leg is hurting him. Will you stay and listen to the choir practice?"

Sam frowned. "Don't I get enough of that in church? Besides, I have chores to do down at the barn and I also have to do some of Dad's chores, too, until his leg's better."

Sherry smiled. He was his father's son. "Okay. Say hi to the frogs for me."

JONATHAN FULLY INTENDED to lie in bed with his book and his earplugs and totally ignore what was going on in the rest of the house. But he couldn't seem to get into his novel, though it was one he'd been looking forward to, a historical war epic by one of his favorite authors. He was acutely aware of the sound of furniture being moved, and most especially of Sherry's voice and occasional bursts of laughter.

He liked her laugh. Though her voice was high and soft, her laugh was almost boisterous, involving her whole body when she did it.

Thinking of Sherry's body was the last thing he needed. He was in no position to take a cold shower. With dogged determination, he forced himself to read a paragraph about the building of Hadrian's Wall, though he'd read it four times already and couldn't seem to absorb the information.

Finally the battle got under way, and Jonathan managed to read five whole pages before he was jerked out of the story yet again. The singing had started.

Jonathan wondered if he actually had the energy to get up and find some earplugs, but he doubted his search would be successful. When had he ever needed them before? One of the things he loved about living way out in the country was how quiet it was, with just the occasional cow mooing, or dog barking, and the soothing sound of wind or rain.

The singing was awful. He knew the choir was learning a new program for Christmas, so the false starts and sour notes were inevitable. But that was no comfort to his eardrums.

Someone knocked on the bedroom door.

"Who is it?" he asked cautiously, fearing one of

the choir ladies had mistaken his room for the bathroom.

"It's just me," came Sam's voice.

"Come in."

He entered looking a bit glum, then flopped on the end of the bed, though he was careful to avoid Jonathan's injured leg.

"What's up?" Jonathan asked.

"How long are those church ladies going to be here? One of 'em pinched my cheeks. I stayed down at the barn a long time, I did every chore I could think of, but they were still here when I got back."

Jonathan looked at his watch. It was almost nine. "I expect they'll be breaking up soon."

"Dad, how long is Sherry going to stay?"

"Just until Pete and Sally get back from their honeymoon. You're the one who wanted her here, remember?"

"I wasn't complaining. I was just thinking it would be nice if she could stay longer."

"Really?"

"She's fun."

"She invited the choir here," Jonathan reminded his son.

Just then the ladies' voices rose in a beautiful harmony, very different than they'd sounded before. Jonathan and Sam both stopped to listen.

"Wow, it's all of a sudden sounded like angel voices," Sam said in a hushed voice.

The song ended, followed by spontaneous, self-congratulatory applause. "We did it!" someone shouted.

"I think I'll go see if there's any pie left," Sam said, hopping off the bed. "Want me to bring you some?"

Jonathan winced as he remembered the burned cherry pie. "No, thanks."

After Sam left, Jonathan pondered his son's contradictory feelings for Sherry. He'd seemed resentful of her intrusion at first, but she'd quickly won him over. It had been so long since an adult female had lived under this roof. Sam had only been three when Rita left.

Maybe Sam was simply drinking in the female presence. She was the closest thing to a mother figure he'd encountered around here in a long time.

Jonathan laid down his book. He wished he could go to sleep, but his leg throbbed and he itched all over. What he needed was a proper bath. This business of using a washcloth and a sink was for the birds.

The more he thought about being immersed in a tub up to his neck, the steaming water undoing all the kinks in his body, the more he wanted it. He needed to relax so he could sleep, and relaxing never came easily to him.

He could probably manage a bath without getting the cast wet. He could prop his left leg on the side of the tub, maybe wrap the top in plastic to protect it. The trickiest part would be getting in and out of the tub. Fortunately, he had strong arms.

His mind made up, he retrieved his crutches from where they leaned against the nightstand and maneuvered out of bed. The moment he was upright, shooting pains reverberated through his leg. It felt like little gremlins with hammers were inside his shin, beating on the bone while dipping every nerve in acid. Sweat broke out on his forehead.

He made it to the bathroom all right, then sank onto the edge of the tub to run the water. While he was waiting for the water to get hot, he spotted the prescription bottle sitting by the sink. When he'd refused to take any medication yesterday, Sherry had given up and left the bottle in here.

She was right. He could take one, just this one time, so he could get a good night's sleep. While the tub filled, he ran a glass of water from the sink and swallowed one of the orange horse pills.

A few minutes later he stepped one foot into the tub, then gingerly lowered himself into the water. The logistics didn't work quite the way he'd pictured: there was nowhere comfortable to prop his leg where it wasn't contorted at some weird angle. He grabbed a towel off a nearby rack, as well as the bath mat, and folded them up into makeshift bolsters until finally he could rest in relative comfort.

He hadn't heard the choir for a few minutes, he realized. They must have gone home. He felt a little guilty for not at least saying hi. But Sherry had invited them, he reminded himself. It wasn't his gig.

He scrubbed himself with a soapy washcloth until his skin turned pink, thinking no bath had ever been so welcome. Then he eased back in the warm water, closed his eyes and relaxed.

He must have dozed off, because the next thing he realized, the water was cool and his fingertips were wrinkled up like raisins.

"Enough of this," he muttered as he tried to sit up. But he had trouble. His arms and legs felt as if they were full of grits, and his head was spinning. With concentrated effort he managed to get his good leg under him. He retrieved one crutch for support. Now all he had to do was straighten his leg and he was home free. He was about halfway vertical, congratulating himself on his ingenuity, when his foot slipped out from under him. He lost his balance and fell back into the water with a splash that spilled over the sides of the tub. His crutch flew out of his hand, the metal crashing loudly onto the tile floor.

"Goddammit!"

Chapter Six

"Jonathan? Jonathan, what happened? Are you hurt?"

"I'm fine—" But before he could get the assurance out, Sherry had burst into the bathroom, all nursely concern.

"Don't move." She kicked off her shoes, sloshed through the inch of water on the bathroom floor and was by his side in an instant. "Did you hit your head? Does anything hurt?" She gently probed his head and neck, her eyes maintaining a very professional contact with his.

He wanted to tell her that he wasn't hurt, that she and her professionalism could just scoot on out the door and let him recover his dignity, if that were possible. But her hands on him felt so incredibly good that he just didn't say anything. Maybe she would have to examine his entire body with her very clever, very professional hands.

"If you wanted a bath, you should have asked," she scolded.

"I'm tired of asking people for things. Anyway, last time I asked, you said no way." He figured he'd

better say something or she would think he was cat-
atonic and call an ambulance. "And I'm not hurt—"
He groaned.

"Did I find a sore spot?"

"Sherry, I'm fine," he said with more urgency.
"Could you just please leave?" Because if she didn't,
she was going to realize he was aroused. It wasn't as
if he could hide it under the present circumstances.

"And let you slip and fall again? Not in this lifetime. Here, give me your hand."

"You can't support me. I'm—"

"I've moved patients bigger than you, don't
worry."

Reluctantly he gave her his hand. She kept her gaze
firmly on his as she provided support. He performed
the same maneuver, and once again he almost gained
his feet. But then *her* foot slipped, and they both fell
back into the tub, creating another tidal wave.

Sherry's blouse was instantly soaked—and instantly transparent. She appeared to be wearing a very
plain bra underneath, but her nipples puckered
through both layers of fabric.

"Oh, my gosh, I'm so sorry!" She sputtered
through a few more apologies as she tried to extricate
herself from the tub, but she was having difficulty,
which might have been explained by the fact that Jonathan had his arms around her. He wasn't sure how
they'd gotten there. This whole scene had taken on a
dreamlike feeling.

"Maybe we ought to just stay here," he said,
hardly believing the words had come out of his
mouth. But suddenly he couldn't bear to have her

move away from him. She was every bit as soft and warm and womanly as he'd imagined, and she smelled incredible.

"Uh, Jonathan..." But she stopped struggling. Her barely peach-tinted lips, so moist and inviting, were parted slightly as she gasped for breath. Was she as excited as he was? One way to find out. He put a hand behind her head, buried his fingers in her hair and pulled her mouth to his.

SHERRY COULDN'T BELIEVE this was happening. How had she *let* it happen? More to the point, how could she stop it? She felt helpless to halt the kiss, which was everything she'd ever wanted in a kiss. Here she'd thought Jonathan was so immune to her, so detached, and yet she'd unwittingly unleashed a deep well of passion.

She returned the kiss in full measure. She just couldn't help herself. Though this had to be the most awkward and uncomfortable position she'd ever been in with a man, she made no move to get out of it.

They must have been kissing for several minutes, neither of them uttering a word, when Sherry felt Jonathan shiver. It might have been a shiver of passion, but she suspected he was getting chilled in his cooling bath water, and so was she.

Determinedly she broke off the kiss. "We have to move."

"Mmm. If we move, are you going to get all professional on me?"

"Well, you *are* my patient—"

He cut off her objection by kissing her again. "I

am not your patient, except in a very occasional and transitory way. I hired you to cook, clean and take care of my children."

She gasped at the reminder. "Sam!"

"He's in bed, isn't he?"

"Yes, I sent him to bed a while ago, but if he heard the crash—"

"He didn't. That kid could sleep through an earthquake."

"But—"

Jonathan kissed her again. She wasn't going to win this battle. She'd never been very good at denying her body what it wanted, and right now it wanted Jonathan. Deep down, wasn't this what she'd been hoping for? That Jonathan would notice the new Sherry and respond?

He shivered again.

"Okay, that's it, mister. We're getting out of this tub."

"And then what?"

"I haven't a clue." She'd never seen this teasing side of Jonathan. It made him that much harder to resist.

"I'll get out of the tub if you'll promise not to run off." He captured her wrist and held it lightly.

"O-okay." She wasn't committing to anything, she reasoned.

Somehow she managed to climb out of the tub. She threw a towel on the floor to sop up some of the water and provide traction. Then, between them, they got Jonathan on his feet and out of the bath.

She handed him a dry towel from a stack sitting

on the hamper, then got one for herself. As she blotted her clothes, she realized her blouse was completely see-through.

Jonathan pulled the towel from her hands, dropped it on the floor and advanced on her with amazing agility for a man with only one good leg. He backed her up against the sink. "Now, where were we?"

"I was about to say this is very unprofessional of me—" She dodged the kiss he would have used to shut her up.

"I didn't hire you as a nurse," he reminded her.

"You're still my employer."

His hands went to the top of her blouse, where he flicked open one button. "Only for a few more days."

"But this is crazy!" she blurted out.

"Why?" He undid the second button.

She could have told him to stop, and she knew he would have. But somehow the request never crossed her lips. "I'm sure Jeff and Allison have told you all sorts of things about me—that I'm a flirt, that I chase men, that I'm easy—"

"No one said you were easy," he said, though not denying the other two descriptions.

"It's all true." She rushed through her words, try-ing to get everything said before she melted into a puddle of pure need. "I like men. I made a fool of myself over your brother last summer. I've slept with a lot—"

"I don't care." Another button magically came un-done. He kissed the top of the valley between her breasts.

''But there are certain lines I can't cross, for my own peace of mind.''

He raised his head and looked at her. ''Just answer one question. Do you want me? Because if you don't, just say so.''

She couldn't look into those bottomless brown eyes and lie. ''Yes, I want you. But—''

''Then take me. Put me out of my misery. No board of ethics is going to come down and give you a demerit. You're not compromising your work. In fact, I'd say making love with me would have a certain therapeutic value.''

''But—''

''Sherry, you could talk a man to death.'' Her shirt was open all the way down the front now. Jonathan slid his arms inside it and around her ribs, pulling her close for another soul-searing kiss. When he was finished, she was gasping for breath. ''So, what'll it be? A night of mindless passion? Or one of lonely misery and regret?''

Hell, when he put it that way, what choice did she have?

''Mindless passion,'' she murmured guiltily.

''Then do you mind if we relocate to the bed? I'm long past the age when I could make love on a tile floor.''

''Oh. Here, let me—''

''I can manage. For this night, Sherry, I want you to forget you're a nurse. Forget I'm writing your paycheck. You're a woman and I'm a man, and that's it.'' He lightly caressed her cheek before turning to exit the bathroom. She was helpless to do anything but follow him like a puppy, taking a long, appreciative, and definitely nonprofessional look at his backside. Maybe she should take up horseback riding, she mused. It was obviously great for toning the butt.

She took a quick detour to the bedroom door, which was wide-open. She closed and locked it. When she turned back to the bed, Jonathan was already sitting on the edge and laying down his crutches. He swung his cast up and onto the mattress, a move that was starting to look practiced. Then he crooked his finger at her.

"Ordinarily I would want to spend a great deal of time and energy undressing you," he said. "But since I'm less than agile at the moment, why don't you take your clothes off for me?"

"Like a striptease?"

"Yes."

For all her experience, Sherry had rarely done anything except make love with the lights off. Despite her continued optimism, her long list of one-night stands had seldom been interested in anything more complex than getting their jollies and departing—quickly.

Certainly she'd never pegged Jonathan as the type to be such a brazen lover. In fact, everything about his behavior tonight had struck her as out of character. He'd probably said more to her in the last few minutes than he had since they'd met.

His suggestion that she strip made her tremble with anticipation. She sauntered up close to the bed, then wordlessly peeled off the wet shirt and tossed it aside. Her jeans came next, and she discovered how difficult it was to remove wet jeans in anything resembling a provocative way. But finally when she was free of them, she stood before Jonathan in nothing but her bra and panties.

She'd *told* Allison and Anne that a sports bra was a bad idea. But at least she was wearing a sexy pair of peach-colored silk panties. She quickly pulled the bra off over her head.

Jonathan's intake of breath was audible. Good.

She turned her back on him and wiggled out of her panties, kicking them aside. Now, all of a sudden, she felt shy. Her timing was impeccably bad.

"Turn around."

She did, and then he did the one thing guaranteed to win over any momentary reluctance: he held out his arms to her. She went to him, climbing carefully into bed so as not to jostle his injured leg. Then he pulled the covers over both of them and just held her close for a few precious seconds.

She felt his arousal against her hip. She wanted to reach down and stroke him, to lay the flat of her hand against his flank and feel those muscles she'd appreciated only a few minutes ago. But she also didn't want to play the brazen hussy. It hadn't escaped her attention that Jonathan hadn't responded to her as a woman until she'd changed her image. Obviously, a more demure-looking and -acting woman was what turned him on.

Then he started kissing her ear, and she didn't worry about her image anymore. She just did what had always come naturally to her—pleasing a man.

Only this time it mattered, more than it ever had before, that she make him happy.

She didn't want this to be another one-night stand, or even a few nights. But realistically what else could it be? They lived and worked so far apart. But there were weekends....

As her mind spun improbable fantasies, her body was busy following its own agenda. She took advantage of Jonathan's hampered mobility, kissing him all over his body while he writhed and groaned and said naughty things to her, encouraging her lascivious activities.

By now any other man would have tired of her teasing, flipped her over on her back, and had his way with her. But Jonathan couldn't, which meant *she* got to decide when and how they conducted their lovemaking. She felt heady with the power.

"This is supposed to be therapeutic," Jonathan said in a husky whisper. "You're going to give me a heart attack."

"I seriously doubt that." She nibbled his ear while stroking his arousal as she'd wanted to do earlier.

But her power was illusory. She'd forgotten how strong he really was. He grabbed her around the waist and hoisted her astride him.

She giggled. "Ride 'em, cowboy, huh?" But she sobered as the evidence of his need pushed against her. Raw desire rose up in her—swift, hot, demanding. "Jonathan. I forgot to ask. Shoot, hell, damn, I'm not protected."

He grinned. "Hell of a time to think of that. Don't worry. I'm healthy and I won't get you pregnant."

"Then how do you explain Sam and Kristin?"

"I had the, er, operation. Rita didn't want any more kids."

Sherry knew she was supposed to feel relieved that she wasn't risking an unplanned pregnancy. Instead she felt a sinking sensation. Jonathan couldn't have more children. With her.

Her concerns were ridiculous, and she did her best to brush them aside. She was getting way ahead of herself if she was already thinking about marriage and kids. But then, that was what she always did.

"Sherry? That doesn't bother you, does it?"

She smiled slowly as she realized she had better things to do than worry about Jonathan's fertility. Much better things.

She was more than ready to take him into her. As he pushed her against him and slowly entered, she sighed with pleasure. He filled her so perfectly. This felt like more than sex. It felt like completion, like the last two pieces of a particularly difficult jigsaw puzzle.

The foreplay had been agonizingly slow, but the crescendo they'd been building toward came far too quickly for Sherry. It wasn't Jonathan's fault. She was just so incredibly aroused, it took very little stimulation to send her leaping off a cliff. She was free-falling at about a million feet per second, the ride more thrilling than any roller coaster.

When her body stilled and her true environment reasserted itself, she found herself in Jonathan's arms. He was stroking her hair and murmuring sweet nothings to her. She realized he must have had his moment, too, otherwise he wouldn't be so still and quiet.

"I...I think I blacked out there for a moment," she said.

"You sure went somewhere. So did I."

She took a deep, cleansing breath. "This was crazy."

"Shh. No regrets. It sure felt like the right thing to do. Still does."

He was correct about that.

"I guess Allison and Anne were right," she said.

"About what?"

"About what you'd like. Now, I don't want you to think I changed myself because I wanted to get you into bed. But I did want you to respect me, to think of me as someone who could competently care for you and your children."

He shifted her from atop him to beside him, nuzzling her hair. "You've got it bass ackward, darlin'. I liked you better before the big makeover."

"But..." Now that didn't make just a whole lot of sense. "You said I didn't fit in, that I was cheap and flashy."

He lifted his head and looked at her, taking exception. "I said nothing like that. I said you were a lousy cook and a poor disciplinarian, and that you didn't belong in a small town."

"Well, there you have it."

"And you know why I said all those things?"

"Because my casserole almost poisoned you, I couldn't handle your kids and your friends and relatives think I'm scandalous?"

"Because I was so hot for you I had a hard time keeping my hands off you. I was looking for any excuse to send you packing because I didn't want to face my own needs."

"Then…you don't like the preacher's daughter image?"

He paused before answering. "I think you're beautiful no matter what you do to yourself. But I'd be lying if I said all that blond hair and tight clothes and spike heels didn't turn me on."

Sherry laughed, savoring the compliment. *Beautiful.* "So trashy-looking women turn you on?"

"Trashy isn't the right word. Let's just say 'the natural look' was never my favorite."

"I did get it wrong, then. Still…" She turned onto her side and propped her head on her hand so she could see his face. "My image did need a change. I didn't see it until Anne and Allison explained it to me. I *was* a little too much. Dressing up like a sex pot is fine if I'm going out on the town, but in work situations I needed to tone it down."

"Sherry, you dress in whatever way you think is best. It doesn't matter to me. Obviously the preacher's daughter look wasn't much of a deterrent."

She lay back down, liking his answer. It implied that there was something about her besides her looks that made him want to take her to bed. She'd relied on her face and body to attract males since she was twelve years old. She would need to shift her thinking a bit.

When she found herself dozing off, she shook herself awake and reluctantly crawled out from the warmth of Jonathan's bed.

He stirred. "Where are you going?"

"I think I should sleep in my own bed. It wouldn't do for Sam to find me here."

"He won't. He sleeps soundly and he doesn't wake up until I wake him up to go to school."

"You're sure?"

"Stay the night. Stay at least some of the night."

Gratefully she slid back under the covers. She'd been given a rare gift—snuggling the entire night, or most of it. She determined she would stay awake as long as she could, savoring each moment, because she had no idea what Jonathan's attitude toward her might be tomorrow.

SHERRY AWOKE to the sound of Jonathan's soft, even breathing and the first light of dawn peeking through the shades. She couldn't remember the last time she felt this content.

Don't get used to it, she cautioned herself. She'd never been the type to inspire loyalty in a man. Not that she didn't want to. Like most women, she fantasized about hearth and home, a white picket fence, anniversaries, children.

Especially children.

It was only in quiet, unguarded moments like this that she let herself dwell on the child she'd given up. Brandon would be twelve years old now. She'd give anything to see him, to know if he was happy. She'd written a letter to him when she'd given him up for adoption, which was kept in a file. If Brandon ever came seeking information about his birth parents, the letter would be given to him and he could initiate contact if he chose. She always kept her contact information up to date with the adoption agency, just in case.

She wondered what he looked like. Brandon's father, Don, had hung around only long enough to give her his DNA. But he'd been a good-looking cuss, tall and slim and blond. She imagined Brandon taking after him.

She'd wanted to keep him. Initially she'd decided she would. But then her parents went to work on her. She'd been nineteen, not a child, and had just completed her first year of junior college. The only way she'd been able to go to school full-time was by living at home, detestable as that situation was. And she'd wanted an education more than anything. All she had to do was look at her mother to see what kind of future awaited her if she didn't get the training she needed to make a decent living.

Her parents threatened to kick her out of the trailer when she refused to give up her child. But she held her ground, and they never carried through on their threat. She'd been paying for groceries and a few bills with her pitiful part-time waitressing income, and they didn't want to lose that.

But they bided their time. They waited until she was in the hospital, having the baby, before they put the real pressure on. They'd had an adoption agency draw up papers. And if she didn't sign away her parental rights to Brandon, then she need not bother coming home to the trailer.

A bleak future had presented itself to Sherry. If she kept Brandon, she would be out on the street, forced to take temporary refuge at a homeless shelter. There would be no one to care for Brandon while she worked or went to school. What kind of life would she be providing for her child? She would be exposing him to danger, health risks and a life of poverty.

For three days her parents reminded her of this on a constant basis. And then the lady from the adoption agency paid her a visit, so kind and well meaning yet so unremitting with her assurances that Brandon would be adopted by a loving couple, with money and a nice home, thoroughly investigated for their fitness as parents.

The situation seemed hopeless. For once in her life, Sherry had lost her fighting spirit. She signed the papers and had regretted it ever since.

Looking back, she realized her parents had pulled a real snow job on her. She wasn't the only single mother in the world. She could have kept Brandon. It would have been hard at first, but there were social programs set up for young, single mothers in trouble. She could have gotten back on her feet, gotten a full-time job, found child care. Moms did it all the time. Eventually she could have continued her education, albeit more slowly. Once Brandon was in school, she could have followed her dream to become a nurse. By now, she would have her certificate.

But she'd suffered from tunnel vision and she'd made the wrong decision.

Mere weeks after coming home from the hospital without Brandon, she'd moved out on her own, anyway. Her relationship with her parents, never strong to begin with, had become so strained she feared for her safety. She and another teenage girl had shared a tiny dump of an apartment. Sherry had continued her education, gone to nursing school, made a life for herself. But always there was a hole. There would always be a hole and not even a night with sexy Jonathan Hardison could fill it.

The room was growing brighter. With a sigh she got out of bed, trying not to disturb Jonathan. He was sleeping soundly, and Lord knew he needed the sleep.

Her clothes, strewn all over the room, were still damp. Ugh. She went to the closet and found a plaid flannel robe in the very back. It swallowed her, but it would do. She paused in front of Jonathan's dresser, then ran her finger along the wood surface. It was dusty. The cleaning service was supposed to come today, she realized, so though she felt compelled to rush back in here with a can of Pledge, she would resist.

She started to turn toward the door when something sparkly caught her eyes. Even in the dim light, the object captured Sherry's attention. When she picked it up, she realized it was an antique tortoiseshell comb encrusted with gemstones.

It was beautiful, a truly stunning piece. Sherry had always loved combs. She liked to twist her hair into elaborate contortions and hold it in place with an unusual accessory that would start conversations. But she'd never owned one this wonderful.

What was it doing on Jonathan's dresser? The conclusion she reached was depressing. She wasn't the first lady friend to visit Jonathan's bedroom in recent history. Whoever had forgotten it would probably be back for it, and soon.

But not before Sherry had a chance to try it out. She'd slept on her damp hair, and it was curlier and wilder than ever. She grabbed a handful of curls, twisted them loosely onto the crown of her head, then stuck the comb into place. She turned her head this way and that, admiring the effect.

JONATHAN OPENED ONE EYE, saw a woman posing in front of the mirror and for a moment, thought he'd gone back in time to when he was married. Then he realized the woman wasn't Rita, but Sherry. His nurse.

Memories of the previous night flooded his consciousness, and he stifled a groan. What in the hell had he done? He remembered falling in the tub, remembered making an ungodly racket with his crutches. Then Sherry had rushed in to rescue him…and he'd jumped her like a randy teenager.

It wasn't that he couldn't remember what had happened. In fact, he recalled every detail, every slimy line of dialogue he'd used to coax her into bed, every trick of seduction he'd ever used or heard of. But he remembered it as if watching the scene through a lens covered with Vaseline. And the man in that scene hadn't resembled Jonathan in the slightest.

Had aliens invaded his body last night? Not that he hadn't enjoyed making love to Sherry. He couldn't remember ever enjoying sex to that degree, even with his lack of agility. But he must have been out of his mind to act on his fantasies, never mind Jeff's advice. Now he had a complicated mess on his hands. What would she expect? What was called for? How was he supposed to handle it? Casual sex wasn't part of his repertoire.

It must have been that damn pain pill. He *knew* there was a reason he shouldn't have taken it. It had relaxed him to the point of removing every one of his inhibitions.

More fully awake now, he watched Sherry fiddling with her hair, her wonderful, abundant hair. He wished she hadn't cut it, but it still turned him on.

Slowly he began to realize exactly what she was doing. She was trying on Rita's comb. Like a cold waterfall, Jonathan was bombarded with all the reasons he didn't need to get himself involved with a high-maintenance woman. He'd purposely left the comb on his dresser as a daily reminder of the pain one such woman brought into his life.

"What are you doing?" The question came out louder, more accusing than he intended.

Sherry whirled around, a guilty look on her face. The comb winked at him from atop her head. "I, um…"

"Put the comb back where you found it, please."

Sherry yanked the comb from her hair and laid it on the dresser. Without another word she ducked her head and fled the room.

"Way to go, Hardison," he muttered to himself. He'd made Sherry cry. Again.

Chapter Seven

Sherry stood in the shower for a good twenty minutes trying to calm down. She was overreacting. He'd told her to put the comb down; he hadn't told her to get out of his room, to never touch his things, to leave him alone or to forget they'd ever had sex. He'd simply asked her to put the comb down.

It was his tone of voice, though, that had done Sherry in. He hadn't spoken in the tone of a lover. Nothing about his voice had indicated fondness. He'd been irritated with her. Probably wearing his robe had been a mistake, too, but she couldn't very well walk naked down the hall when Sam slept only a few feet away. She would wash the robe, press it and return it to his closet at the first opportunity.

Why did she always do this? Why did she go to bed with a guy, investing all of herself wholeheartedly into the experience? Why did she bother spinning fantasies about the future, when she knew that with men it was always about sex? Just sex. She'd been available and willing. That was usually all it took.

Why couldn't she look at it that way, too? The sex

had been incredible, mind-blowing. It had been a wonderful experience. Why couldn't she just accept that it was a one-time deal, savor the memories and move on? But no, she had to bring her stupid emotions into the equation and muck everything up.

If she could pack up and leave, she would. But Jonathan was still her patient. What was more, Kristin would be coming home soon and she would need Sherry's nursing skills. She could not in good conscience abandon the Hardisons, no matter how much she wanted to.

She would only have to endure this situation for a few more days, until Pete and Sally came home from their cruise. Somehow she would get through it.

After her shower, Sherry was faced with the dilemma of what to wear. To be honest, she hadn't really liked the country-mouse look. But if she tricked herself up the way she usually did, Jonathan would think she was doing it for him.

Maybe a compromise was in order. She selected a pair of snug black jeans and a zebra-print sweater with a V-neck that was a bit clingy, but not too revealing, especially if she wore another sports bra. For shoes she chose a pair of black leather clogs. Not spike heels, but not boring sneakers, either. Taming the curl out of her hair was too much trouble, so she skipped that step, but she didn't tease it up, either. She pulled the front part back into a clip, which looked sort of sedate. She toned down her usual makeup, but not to where she looked invisible, as she had yesterday.

She put a pair of faux-diamond studs in her ears. Eye-catching, but not overwhelming.

When she was finished, she felt pleased with the results. She definitely wasn't a country mouse. Let Jonathan make of it what he would.

As she left her bedroom, a delectable smell drifted from the kitchen. Someone was cooking? She glanced at her watch, realizing she was running late. When she entered the kitchen, she found Jonathan pulling a golden-brown waffle from a waffle iron.

"Jonathan!" she objected. "What are you—you're not supposed to—"

"It won't kill me to be standing for a few minutes," he said calmly. "I missed making Sunday breakfast yesterday, so I thought I'd make up for it today. Sam always looks forward to my waffles."

He hopped a few steps over, using the countertop for support and retrieved a bowl of batter. He poured the remainder of the batter into the waffle iron, closed it, then set the bowl in the sink.

Sherry darted to the sink. "Here, let me at least do that part." Stubborn man. But he must be feeling better to attempt such an ambitious project.

He hopped back to the table and sat down while he waited for the last waffle to cook. Three others were stacked on a plate nearby. Maple syrup, strawberries, canned whipped cream, and crumbled pecans were assembled on the table, which was set with three place settings.

Sherry didn't know quite what to make of the homey scene, so out of sync with what had happened a few minutes ago.

"I'll go get Sam," she said after rinsing the bowl and putting it in the dishwasher. This whole thing was weird, surreal, as if Jonathan was trying to pretend last night never happened. And maybe he was.

He grabbed her hand as she started to pass, halting her. "Sam will be along shortly. Waffles always hurry him to the table. You sit down. Let me wait on you for a change."

"But that's not—"

"Sit."

She sat. A few moments later the third waffle was ready. Jonathan plucked it from the iron and put it with the others, then brought the stack of waffles to the table.

"You like your waffles loaded?" he asked.

"Sure, I guess." She hadn't eaten waffles in years.

"Then let me fix one up for you."

He sure was being nice. A consolation prize because he didn't want a relationship with her? Some consolation.

Sam came into the kitchen, his shirttail untucked, shoes untied. "I want everything on mine but nuts," he said.

"Please," she corrected absently.

"Oh, yeah. Please," Sam obligingly said.

"Coming right up." Jonathan went to work on both waffles at once. Sherry saw there was a pot of coffee already brewed, so she busied herself pouring cups for herself and Jonathan, and getting a glass of milk for Sam.

"Dig in," Jonathan said as she sat down again and he placed her waffle in front of her. She picked up her fork and started to cut the waffle. That was when she realized the whipped cream had been applied in the shape of a heart.

Startled, she thought she must be imagining things. She glanced over at Sam's waffle. His whipped cream was just a blob in the center. She looked back at her waffle. Definitely a heart.

She tried to catch Jonathan's gaze, but he wasn't looking at her. Was that a hint of a blush on his face?

A rush of sentimental warmth radiated from Sherry's core outward. Jonathan was apologizing for sniping at her, in his own weird way. The gesture was so sweet, so unlike the taciturn Jonathan she thought she knew, it brought tears to her eyes. She blinked them back before anyone could notice.

"Hey, where's my *heart?*" Sam asked.

"What?" Jonathan looked at Sam's waffle, then Sherry's. "Oh, sorry. Got them mixed up." He quickly switched the two plates, then said in an embarrassed tone, "I always put hearts on the kids' waffles."

Now Sherry felt her own face burning. Of *course* the heart wasn't for her. She was such an idiot. She took a bite of the waffle, not even tasting it.

"Eat up," Jonathan said to his son. "The bus will be here soon."

Sam obligingly stuffed half a waffle into his mouth, washed it down with several gulps of milk and jumped up from the table. "Gotta get my backpack."

Sherry continued to eat, avoiding Jonathan's gaze. She wished she could dispense with her waffle as easily as Sam had.

"Do you want seconds?" Jonathan asked.

"No, thanks. It's good, though," she added. Just because things were awkward between them was no reason not to show good manners.

Sam ran out the front door, his jacket half on, shouting goodbye.

"He doesn't like missing the bus, I take it," Sherry said.

"Nope. I make him walk. Oh, don't look at me like I'm an ogre. It's less than two miles."

"And how often does that happen?"

"It's only happened once. That was enough. I believe children—everyone, actually—shouldn't be spared from the consequences of their actions."

"I know, but he's just a little—" She made herself shut up. She was too lenient with the children; at least, Jonathan thought so. If she'd raised children of her own, she probably would have messed them up like her parents had messed her up. She wouldn't know good parenting if it bit her on the nose.

She did what she always did when she was nervous: she started cleaning. She gathered up the dishes, rinsed them at the sink and then put them in the dishwasher. Next, she put away the syrup, ran a sponge over the waffle iron, put it away, then scrubbed down the countertop and table. Finally she swept up the crumbs around the table.

Jonathan watched her, seemingly amused. "You're very good at that. You can stop now, though. The cleaning service will be here in a few minutes."

"You could have reminded me of that five minutes ago." Sherry put the broom away. Now what was she supposed to do? "I should check your leg. How does it feel?"

"It's healing up fine. My toes don't tingle and they're the right color. My head's not spinning and I don't have a temperature. Stop worrying."

"I'll bet there's laundry—"

"You did laundry yesterday."

"Well then, what do you want me to do?" she asked, exasperated. "You're the boss."

With a mischievous smile he grabbed her arm and pulled her into his lap, then wrapped his arms around her.

"Jonathan!"

"I guess this makes me guilty of sexual harassment, huh?" He nuzzled her neck, which made it hard for her to think.

"You're guilty of acting like a maniac." But part of her was thrilled. He wasn't going to just brush her off, pretend nothing had happened. And neither was she.

It would have been so easy just to twist around, wind her arms around his neck and kiss him. She turned to jelly whenever he touched her. But a little voice inside her head, one that was usually absent, was screaming at her to show caution for a change. She pulled away from him and got to her feet.

"No. No, this just isn't right."

"Sherry—"

"You don't just yell at someone, then five minutes later pretend it never happened." Sherry wasn't sure what had come over her. She couldn't remember the last time she'd stood up to a man, any man. Usually she just did whatever it took to stay in a man's good graces for however long it lasted. But not today, not with Jonathan. She felt too strongly about him, and about his treatment of her, to just let it slide.

"I'm sorry I raised my voice. It was uncalled-for."

Sherry had never heard a more perfunctory apology in her life. Still, he'd apologized. That was something. Many men never mastered that skill.

"I don't like being yelled at," she said. "What's the deal with the comb? Does it belong to a girlfriend?" Might as well get this out in the open now. She cringed inwardly, waiting for his answer.

"I don't have a girlfriend. The comb belonged to my mother. And it briefly belonged to my wife."

Ah. Now she understood, or at least she thought she did. By playing with the comb, she had encroached on sacred territory—his wife. He hadn't referred to her as his ex-wife, either. Obviously, he still cared for her, or he wouldn't keep the comb around to remind him of her.

The message couldn't be clearer. Jonathan wanted Sherry, wanted her in his bed, maybe for even more than just one night. He might even be fond of her, but she had her place and she'd better stay in it.

"You don't appear to be in a very forgiving mood," Jonathan said.

She sighed. "Of course I forgive you. I'm about the most forgiving person you'll ever run across. But that doesn't mean I want to jump back into bed with you. Not while I'm working for you. You joke about sexual harassment, but I've had problems with it in the past and it's no fun."

"Surely you know I would never make your employment conditional on—"

"You fired me because you found me attractive."

"And I admitted that was a mistake. Besides, I've found a much better way of dealing with my attraction."

If he didn't stop looking at her like that, her bones were going to melt. She steeled herself to say what she knew she had to say, what she knew was right. "I'm asking that we cool things for a while. When Pete and Sally come home and I'm no longer working for you, we can revisit the issue."

"Revisit the issue?"

"Talk about having a relationship."

"But you'll be leaving."

"Dallas isn't that far away. Anyway, I'll be leaving at the end of the week. If you just want to sleep with me because I'm here and I'm convenient, and you intend to forget about me the moment I'm out of sight, then frankly I'm just not interested. I've had my fill of one-night stands. I don't want to be some guy's temporary toy. I want a real relationship, something with a little substance, not a wisp of steam that'll disappear at the first sign of wind."

He looked her over, as if he was seeing her for the first time. "You look good in that sweater."

"Are we agreed?" She refused to be distracted. "No more hanky-panky while I'm living under your roof, caring for you and your children."

Finally he nodded. "You're right. Things got a little crazy last night. We should slow down, anyway."

She wasn't sure she liked his response, but the

doorbell rang, giving her an excuse to escape from the kitchen. She opened the door to two plump, middle-aged women with a "Sharon's Personal Service" insignia on the breast pockets of their uniforms. A van parked in the driveway said the same thing.

Sherry smiled at them, as they looked puzzled. "Hi, I'm Sherry, Mr. Hardison's...nurse."

"Oh, that's right," one of the women said. "We heard he had an accident." They stepped inside. Jonathan waved at them from the doorway to the kitchen.

"How're you doing, Mr. Jonathan?" the second woman asked.

"Pretty well, Esther, thanks. I'll be in the den, ladies, if you need anything."

The women made themselves right at home, cleaning like a couple of whirling dervishes, which left Sherry with nothing to do. After some debate, she went into the den, also, where she found Jonathan puttering on a computer. He was looking at weather reports for the region.

Sherry adopted her most serious, professional demeanor. "Jonathan, is there something I should be doing? I feel useless."

"There is something you could do," he said, matching her emotionless tone. "I've tried a couple of times this morning to rouse someone down at the barn. But no one answers the phone there or the cell phone. Could you try to find Wade or Cal, and ask 'em to call?"

"Sure."

He tossed her a set of keys. "The four-wheeler is

by the back door, and those keys should get you through any gates that are locked.''

''A four-wheeler? You mean like an ATV? I've never driven one of those before.''

''There's nothing to it. You'll figure it out.'' He turned back to the computer, dismissing her.

This was what you wanted, remember? Right about then, Sherry wanted to tell that little voice in her head to shove it. Had she made the right decision? Wouldn't it have been better to have Jonathan for a few days than not at all, never again?

But for the first time in her life, her answer to that question was no. She was done compromising. Sleeping with a guy before she really knew him had caused more problems in her life than she could count. Things would be different from now on.

Maybe the makeover had worked on something besides her physical appearance, she thought as she headed out the back door, intent on tackling the four-wheel vehicle, which looked like an overgrown toy to her.

ONCE SHERRY WAS SAFELY out of the house, Jonathan turned off his computer. He hadn't been able to concentrate on it, anyway. All he could think about was the amazing creature who'd stood in his kitchen and spoken words like ''relationship.'' Clearly this was not a woman to be trifled with.

Perhaps he *had* been trifling with her, he reflected. He'd told Jeff he wasn't into one-night stands. But had he really intended to get involved with Sherry?

Absolutely not. She was trouble. She was a complication he didn't need. But to use her to slake his long-dormant desires was wrong. She might dress like a woman who only wanted to tumble into bed, but that wasn't what she really wanted at all. She wanted a "relationship," God help him.

The correct course of action was amazingly easy to plot. He would stay away from her for the remainder of the week, which he really hadn't been given a choice on. Then, when Pete and Sally returned from their honeymoon, he would thank Sherry for doing a terrific job. He would apologize again for all of the stupid things he said and did. He would tell her how honored he was that she'd spent the night with him.

Then he would tell her that he didn't think it was practical for them to have a relationship. He didn't have much to offer in that department. He was still so scarred from his marriage that he didn't believe in love or happily ever after, at least not for him. In the end, they would bring each other nothing but heartache. He would wish her well in finding a partner who deserved someone as special as her.

That was the plan, and it was a good one. The problem was, there wasn't a chance in hell he would actually carry it through. All he could think about was that soon she would no longer be under his employ, and he could make love to her again. He could take her out on a date—he was getting along pretty well with the crutches—maybe take her to Bremond's Steak House, then check into a motel and do all the things he'd been fantasizing about.

Of course, if he did all that, he would be in a relationship with her, whether he wanted to be or not. She'd set up the rules, and he had to follow them.

Hell, maybe it wouldn't be so bad.

THE FOLLOWING WEEK went smoothly enough. On Tuesday Sherry dutifully asked Jonathan if she could invite a small group of dancers to the house that evening. She'd met them at the wedding reception and they'd promised to show Sherry one of their routines.

"What kind of dancers?" Jonathan asked.

"Cloggers," she admitted. "But we'll go out on the patio. It won't bother you."

He had reluctantly agreed. When the six women arrived that night, Jonathan made a point of greeting them. He even poked his head out on the patio to see what they were up to, but hastily retreated when they asked if he wanted to watch.

On Wednesday morning it was the quilters. They came over for lunch, then showed Sherry the quilt they were working on and allowed her to sew some stitches. It seemed Sherry wanted to bond with everyone in town, and her mind was open to every new experience that came her way.

Kristin came home from the hospital Wednesday afternoon, expecting to be treated like a princess, and everyone obliged. Even Sam was especially nice to her, bringing her lessons home from school and helping her with her spelling, letting her play with his coveted Game Boy Advance, sharing the last of his Halloween candy hoard.

Sherry prepared all Kristin's favorite foods and brought them to her on a tray. She kept an eye on

Kristin's physical condition, administered her prescription medicines, cleaned and dressed her incision, watched insipid videos with her.

Kristin also was favored with visits from her grandfather, her uncles and Aunt Anne and baby cousin Olivia, and almost-Aunt Allison. Even Rita called to see how she was doing. Jonathan had dutifully informed Rita of Kristin's illness. And though his ex-wife hadn't rushed to be by their daughter's side, she had seemed genuinely distressed over the news and had made Kristin feel loved and worried over with her phone call. She'd also Fed-Exed a big white teddy bear.

"We're turning her into a spoiled brat," Jonathan said to Sherry on Thursday as she fixed Kristin her second root-beer float of the day.

"It's just for a few days. You know how miserable it is being confined. As soon as she's up and around, she'll be so happy she won't even miss all the extra attention. She's been talking nonstop about riding her pony."

"Hah! She'll be impossible to live with. Of course, you'll never know. You'll waltz out of here tomorrow and leave us to live with the consequences." He was just teasing, and fortunately she knew it. But he was also trying to get an idea of what her plans were. Would she rush back to Dallas? She had another week before her job with the plastic surgeon started. It'd be nice if she stuck around in Cottonwood.

Sherry just gave him an oblique look, which told him exactly nothing. He could come out and ask her, but he didn't want to seem too eager.

He wasn't being careful because he worried she might reject him. His real concern was that he not promise what he couldn't deliver. He was still getting used to the idea of something more than short-term with Sherry, and he didn't want her to get the idea he was ready to make commitments.

Hell, he was a long way off from that.

But he also didn't want to lose her by being too cagey.

"I talked to Granddad this morning," he said casually. "They're flying out of Miami tomorrow afternoon, so they'll be home before dinner."

"I should fix something special for them. I understand Sally is an excellent cook, so I suppose she'll be making most of the meals. But I don't think she should be pressed into service her first night here."

"No. I'd like you to stay one more night, if you could. Just so Pete and Sally can relax their first evening home."

Sherry nodded her agreement. "They'll probably be exhausted. I don't mind staying till Saturday."

"And then what?"

She halted on her way out of the kitchen to take Kristin her float. "That kind of depends on you."

"I'd like you to stay a few more days. You're welcome to stay here, but if you're worried about appearances, I'm sure Allison would let you stay with her."

"Allison hasn't asked. And yes, it would be awkward for me to stay here."

"Allison will ask, I promise. Otherwise, there's a

perfectly nice bed-and-breakfast on the square. I'll pay for it.''

''I don't want to be your kept woman,'' she bristled.

''Jeez, Sherry, just tell me what I'm supposed to do. I'm rusty at this, as you can probably tell. Are there certain words I'm supposed to say that I'm not?''

In a quicksilver change of mood, Sherry laughed. Then she set the float down, came over and hugged him. ''I'm every bit as clueless as you.''

''One of us should have an idea.''

''I'll ask Allison if I can stay with her a few days. You're right, she won't mind. She's invited me before.''

''Then do you want to go out to dinner Saturday? Or how about a movie? Or we could do both.''

''Whatever you'd like is fine with me.''

''In that case…perhaps you'd better let go of me before I forget myself and ravage you right here on the kitchen table.''

Sherry dutifully stepped away from him. ''Yes sir, boss man.'' With a saucy sway to her hips, she left the kitchen, with the rapidly melting float in hand.

SHERRY COULD HARDLY SLEEP that night. She'd told Jonathan what she wanted, and he was giving it to her. Could it possibly be this simple? Had she lost out on having a decent relationship in the past simply because she hadn't made it clear that was what she wanted? She'd never been coy when it came to sex, but when it came to matters of the heart she'd always been more confused than anything.

If she'd asked Brandon's father to marry her, would he have complied? Instead, she'd hung back, pretending it didn't matter all that much to her. And he'd disappeared almost faster than she could blink.

No, it wasn't in any way simple, she decided. Most men ran from anything that smacked of relationship. If Jonathan had asked her to stick around Cottonwood and go out on a date with him, it was because he wanted to be with her, not because she'd performed the magic ritual, said the right words, cocked her hips at just the right angle.

Maybe he'd have been content to simply sleep with her a few times if she hadn't stated very clearly that wasn't an option. But maybe not. Maybe he actually was starting to care for her, or was at least attracted to something other than her bra size.

On Friday morning Sherry called Allison and invited herself to stay in Allie's guest room a few days. Allison seemed delighted.

"Now that you're a free woman, I can take you around and show you stuff," she said excitedly.

"That'd be great. But I have to warn you. I'm staying partly because Jonathan asked me to."

Allison squealed. "I knew it! Jeff thought I was crazy at first when I said I thought there might be some chemistry between you two. But later he agreed with me."

"Don't go reserving the church. We're taking things slowly. Just a dinner date."

"For Jonathan that's the speed of light. He hasn't

dated since he and Rita split up, except one time when I dragged him to a fish-fry to make Jeff jealous. So, do you think it was the makeover?''

''Allie, in all honesty, he liked me better as a sleaze.''

''Really? Oh, Sherry, you weren't a sleaze.''

''I'm rethinking this whole image thing. In fact, I'm rethinking almost everything about my life.''

''Sometimes you have to. Come over whenever you like. I'll buy chocolate and popcorn. We can watch sappy movies and perform Freudian analysis on each other.''

FRIDAY WAS HECTIC as Sherry made preparations for Pete and Sally's homecoming. First she had to fix up Pete's bedroom, make it more inviting for a woman. Then she had to shop for groceries for the special dinner that evening. Kristin's Brownie troop came over that afternoon to visit her and to take a tour of the ranch with Wade and Cal Chandler. Then Sherry provided cookies and punch.

Jonathan didn't even grumble about the invasion of six- and seven-year-olds. He actually joined them and even let some of the little girls sign his cast.

When the doorbell rang, Sherry thought it might be a Brownie straggler. But a strange boy stood on the front porch, stepping from foot to foot and staring awkwardly at her. He was dark-haired, slightly chunky and wore glasses taped together at the nose piece.

''May I help you?'' Sherry asked politely.

The boy laid down a worn backpack and pulled a

piece of purple paper from his pants pocket, handing it to her without a word. He never stopped staring.

Was he mute? Sherry unfolded the paper, hoping it would explain.

It took her a few moments to recognize the handwriting on the paper as her own, though a more childish script from several years ago. It was a letter, dated twelve years earlier, and it began, "Dear Brandon..."

Oh, surely not. It couldn't be. "What's your name?" she asked.

"Chuck. Chuck Woods."

She felt a shiver of relief, but it lasted only a second.

"I used to be Brandon, for about five minutes when I was born. Are you Sherry McCormick?"

Sherry didn't answer. Instead, she did something she'd never done in her life. She fainted.

Chapter Eight

"What the hell—" Jonathan hobbled to the door as fast as his crutches could move him, managing to beat the Brownie leader who also headed for Sherry's inert form. Several of the little girls abandoned their cookies and punch to check out the situation, watching with big eyes full of curiosity.

"I didn't do anything, I swear," said the boy standing at the front door. "She just—she just—"

"It's okay, son." Jonathan said.

"Hey, I'm not your son. At least, I don't think so."

Jonathan ignored the kid as he threw his crutches aside and leaned down to touch Sherry's arm. "Sherry?"

Her eyes fluttered open. She looked at Jonathan, then the Brownie leader, then the boy. "Oh, dear."

"What happened?" the Brownie leader asked as she helped Sherry sit up. "There, now, don't try to move too fast. Are you hurt?"

"I don't think so."

"I think I sent her into shock," the boy said.

Jonathan turned on him. "Who are you? What did you say?"

He shrugged. "I'm her son. She hasn't seen me in twelve years. Maybe I should have called first."

The Brownie leader went pale. She stood, turned toward her troop and clapped her hands. "Okay, time to pack up and leave!"

Some of the Brownies protested, but they started gathering up their things.

Jonathan, reeling a bit from the shock, returned his attention to Sherry. "Are you really okay? Do you want me to call Jeff or my dad?"

She seemed to snap out of the daze she'd been in. "No, no, I'm fine." She scrambled to her feet and brushed off her clothes as the Brownie leader herded her charges out the door.

"Goodbye, Kristin!" they all shouted as they scooted past the boy, who looked on with a slight sneer. Sherry pulled the boy inside and closed the door. Then they all stared at each other for an awkward few moments.

Finally the boy broke the silence. "Pretty nice house." He lightly touched a bronze statue that stood on a table near the door. Then he looked back at Jonathan. "Are you a cowboy?"

"I am. Um, maybe I should leave you two alone for a bit."

Sherry nodded, her face still disturbingly pale. "That would be good."

Good God, could it really be true? Had Sherry abandoned her own child? He'd actually considered the possibility that Sherry wouldn't be interested in him because she might want her own children someday, and he couldn't help. Okay, the concern was in the very, very back of his mind, but it was there. But obviously she didn't want children, if she hadn't kept the one she'd been given.

"C'mon, Kristin," he said gruffly. "Let's go play on the computer."

Kristin, still playing the invalid princess in her robe and bunny slippers, hopped out of her chair and followed her father, giving the newcomer a curious look before disappearing down the hallway.

Sherry waited until she and Chuck were alone. Her son, her baby, was standing right in front of her. She found herself oddly tongue-tied. What could she possibly say at a time like this? She wanted to throw her arms around him, to tell him how very sorry she was that she'd given him up. But the expression on his face stopped her. He studied her with a mixture of surprise and, yes, distaste.

"I'm so happy you're here. I have so much to tell you, so much to ask you! Are you hungry? Do you want some punch and cookies?"

"Got any Coke?"

"Yes, of course, whatever you want," Sherry said. She didn't know what to make of the strange bombshell that had just dropped into her life. Was this odd-looking, brusque-talking boy really Brandon? He looked nothing like she'd pictured, nothing like the pink, sweet-smelling infant she'd held in her arms so briefly.

It must be a mistake. It must be. Yet she prayed it wasn't. Hadn't she fantasized about this moment? Hadn't she yearned for her son to take an interest in her, to come looking for her so she could explain, apologize, make it up to him?

A million questions rolled around in her head. Finally she settled on one as she got out a glass and a bottle of generic cola. "How did you get here? Did your parents bring you? They're not waiting outside, are they?"

Brandon—Chuck—didn't answer her. Instead he took one look at the soda bottle and said, "Yuck, generic. Don't you have real Coke? Or Pepsi?"

She gave him an apologetic look. "This is all we have, unless you want root beer."

He pulled a face. "Naw, I'll take that."

"How about a roast beef sandwich?" When all else failed, be a good hostess.

He nodded. Good. Something else to do with her hands.

"So tell me about yourself. Do you like school? Are you interested in anything special? I always liked science. And art, I liked to draw. What do your adopted parents do? Are they nice? Do you get along with them?" She realized she was babbling.

"I don't have parents."

Sherry dropped the top to the mayonnaise jar, and it clattered to the floor. "What?"

"They died when I was six. Car accident."

"Oh, my God. So…so where do you live? Didn't someone else adopt you?"

"No. Wake up, lady. No one adopts kids unless they're babies. I went into the foster system."

Sherry's hands were shaking so badly she could hardly slap the sandwich together. She put a handful of chips on the plate with the sandwich and set it on the table in front of Chuck. ''I'm sorry. Oh, God, I'm so sorry.'' She didn't know what else to say.

''Yeah, everybody's sorry,'' he mumbled, then stuffed half the sandwich into his mouth.

''There were no grandparents to take you in? No aunts or uncles?''

''Nope. They didn't want me.''

Sherry's eyes filled with tears. This wasn't right, it wasn't fair. She'd given up her child believing she was giving him a better life and even then she'd regretted it. Her only consolation was picturing him living in a big house with loving parents, maybe brothers and sisters and a dog to play with and lots of toys, the best schools. Clearly her fantasy had been far off base.

''So how did you find me?'' she asked.

''My social worker helped me. She went to the adoption agency and they gave her your address and phone number. And the letter you wrote to me.''

''I meant every word in that letter. I really wanted to keep you.''

''Uh-huh.'' Chuck stuffed a handful of chips in his mouth.

''I was homeless,'' she tried again. ''Or I would have been, if I hadn't agreed to give you up.''

He appeared unmoved by her explanation.

''How did you track me down here?'' she asked, just to keep the conversation moving.

''I went to your place, but you weren't there, so I sat down on the front steps to wait. Some neighbor lady saw me there and came over to check me out.''

"Mrs. Peterson?" Sherry's elderly neighbor kept tabs on all that went on in the neighborhood.

Chuck snorted. "I don't know. Just some old biddy. She said you wouldn't be back soon, that you were taking care of some rancher with a broken leg. She didn't know his name, but she knew the town." He took another gargantuan bite of sandwich and talked with his mouth full. "Did you know there are six towns named Cottonwood in Texas?"

"No, I didn't. How did you know which one?"

"This is the closest one, so I tried it first. I called the Chamber of Commerce and asked if they knew about a rancher with a broken leg. He told me all about it, including all about the nurse he'd hired."

Sherry's head was spinning. She still wasn't used to living in a small town, where everybody knew everybody's business and was perfectly willing to share. What if some serial killer had been inquiring about her, instead of a child? Then again, if Mrs. Peterson and the Chamber of Commerce guy hadn't been so talkative, Brandon—Chuck—wouldn't have found her.

"That was a clever bit of detective work," she said. "You must be a smart kid."

"You wouldn't know it from my grades."

"Well, grades don't tell everything." Sherry's grades in school weren't very good, either, until she'd gotten to college and started working at it. "So did someone drive you here?"

"No. I hitched."

Sherry gasped. "You mean you hitchhiked?"

"Yeah, what about it? I do it all the time." He

licked mayonnaise off his fingers. "Can I have another one?"

"Yes, of course." She hopped up to make another sandwich. "Do your parents—your foster parents—know where you are?"

He made a derisive sound. "It's just one lady, and she's got, like, six foster kids. She takes in kids so she can get the money they pay her. She'll never miss me as long as the checks keep coming."

The news sank in. "So you ran away."

He shrugged. "I do it all the time. You would, too, if you had to live in that rat hole of a house. You can't ever get into the bathroom, and when you can, there's never any soap or toilet paper, and I have to share a bed with this other kid who smells like a Dumpster."

Sherry shuddered. This just got worse and worse. If the conditions he described were real, she couldn't blame him for running away.

"Still, maybe you better call your foster mother and let her know you're safe."

Chuck rolled his eyes. "Then they'll just send me back there."

"But you can't—" She stopped herself. She'd been about to tell him he couldn't stay here. But what message would that send? Just one more person who didn't want him, didn't care about him, considered him a nuisance?

He looked at her with accusing eyes. "So you don't want me, either."

"No, no, it's not that," she said hastily. "But this isn't my house. I'd like to spend time with you, get to know you, but I can't just keep you. There are laws we have to follow.'' And if she didn't notify someone soon of Chuck's presence, she could be considered guilty of kidnapping. ''I imagine you're also supposed to be in school.''

''So that means you're sending me back.''

''Gosh, Bran—Chuck. I don't know what to do.'' She gave him the second sandwich, which he devoured as hungrily as he had the first. Maybe his foster mother didn't feed him enough. Then again, he hardly looked malnourished.

She wouldn't say he looked healthy, though. He had that pasty, pudgy look of children who had poor nutrition—too much junk food—and who spent way too much time indoors in front of the television. Early in her nursing career, she'd worked at a public health agency, so she was familiar with the look. Such children often came from impoverished backgrounds.

''Look,'' Chuck said after draining his second glass of cola, ''I'll just save you the trouble. You obviously don't want me around, either, so I'll hit the road.''

''No! I can't let you do that. It's dangerous out there for a child.''

He snorted again. ''I can take care of myself. I been doin' it awhile, you know.''

Her heart went out to him. What had this child suffered? She'd heard horror stories about foster homes. She knew many foster parents were loving and generous and provided safe and comfortable havens for children. But she also knew of the other kind, who took in kids for the very reason Chuck had mentioned—for the money.

"Look, I'll make you a deal," she said. "I'll call your foster mother and let her know where you are, then I'll ask if you can stay the night with me."

He looked dubious. "I dunno…"

"Sam, that's Mr. Hardison's son, has a horse. He might let you ride him," Sherry wheedled.

"How old is this kid?"

"Eight, I think. Third grade."

Chuck snorted, a sound Sherry was becoming familiar with, unfortunately. "I don't think so. But I'll stay if you show me that computer."

"I'll have to ask Mr. Hardison. In fact, I'll have to ask him if you can stay. But he's very nice, and I'm sure he'll say yes. And if he doesn't, well, we'll just go someplace else. Deal?"

"Ask him first."

"Okay." Sherry got up and went to the den, where Kristin sat in front of the computer playing some sort of game that involved bashing gophers on their virtual heads as they popped out of their holes.

Jonathan heard Sherry come in and looked up, a wary expression on his face.

"Would it be all right if Chuck spent the night? He can sleep in my room. I'll let him have my bed. I can sleep on the floor."

"Is it all right with his parents?"

"I'm going to check on all that. I just wanted to clear it with you first."

He nodded, his eyes shuttered. "I have no problem with him staying."

Jonathan turned back to Kristin and her game. "Good one, you got a double."

Was it her imagination, or was Jonathan acting a bit cool toward her? Granted, the situation was awkward at best. Was he judging her because she'd had a child out of wedlock? It wouldn't totally surprise her. He did tend to see things in black and white, right or wrong, his way or no way. But she'd made her mistakes many years ago and learned from them. Surely he could see that.

She returned to the kitchen to find Chuck looking in cabinets.

"I'll get you something else, if you're still hungry," she said. "How about cookies?"

"Store-bought or homemade?"

"Store-bought for now. I could make homemade, though." As if a batch of cookies could make up for twelve years of mothering she'd missed.

"Whatever."

She gave him a handful of chocolate chip mini-cookies, and another of peanut butter cookies. "Mr. Hardison said you can stay. So how about giving me your foster mother's phone number?"

He did, but only reluctantly.

After Sherry dialed, a harried-sounding woman answered. Sherry could hear a child screaming in the background as well as a television, the volume turned up unreasonably loud. "Is this the home of Chuck Woods? I'm looking for his foster mother, Oleta."

"You got her."

Sherry introduced herself and explained the situation. She expected the woman to be breathless with relief that Chuck was safe. But she merely said, "So that's where he went."

"I'd like to keep him overnight, if it's all right with you. I can give you some references—and you can call anyone in town here regarding Mr. Hardison. He's a highly respected—''

"Hey," the woman interrupted. "It's no skin off my nose if you want to keep the little monster for a while. No hurry about returning him."

Sherry was aghast at the woman's attitude. Maybe Chuck hadn't been exaggerating when he'd said his foster mother wouldn't miss him.

"I'll bring him home tomorrow," Sherry said. She figured one day was probably a reasonable length for her first visit with Chuck. She didn't want to overwhelm him. Besides, he didn't have clean clothes with him. "Or you can come pick him up if you prefer."

"Pick him up? Listen, the kid got hisself to Bumpkinville, he can figure out how to get home." With that parting comment, she hung up.

"Told ya," Chuck said. "I could be gone a month and she wouldn't care."

Sherry was very uneasy with this situation. She needed advice. "Maybe I should call your social worker."

"Forget it," Chuck said. "She'll make me go home—or worse, back to the children's home."

"I won't let that happen."

"At least wait a while." Chuck looked at her with pleading eyes, the first sign of vulnerability he'd shown her. "If it's late enough, maybe she'll let me stay 'til morning."

Sherry knew she probably shouldn't wait. Social

Services needed to be notified of this situation, so they could take appropriate measures. But would a few more hours hurt?

Chuck took her indecision as a no. "Ah, hell, you don't want me, either. You never wanted me. I don't know why I thought anything would be different now."

"I did want you," Sherry said passionately.

"Then why'd you give me up?"

She sighed. No answer she gave was going to make him happy. "It wasn't an easy decision. I had no one to turn to for help. I was completely alone, and I didn't think I could possibly be a good mother to you. I wanted more for you, so much more…but I never stopped loving you or wanting to be with you. You were so precious, this tiny little scrap of life, and I was so afraid for you…" The words poured out of her. Twelve years of shame and grief and remorse. She stopped only when tears clogged her throat.

Brandon made no response. In fact, he didn't even look at her.

She dabbed at her eyes with a paper towel. "Is there anything you want to say?" she asked. "Anything you want to ask me?"

He looked around, and for a moment she thought he would open up to her. But then that familiar, cynical look came back into his eyes. "So what's there to do around here?"

Okay, so he didn't want to talk about personal stuff. She'd probably frightened him with her emotional outpouring. She was willing to give him whatever time and space he needed.

With some effort, she pulled herself together. "There are lots of things to do on a ranch. Do you want to go see some horses and cows?"

He shrugged. "I guess." But she could see some interest lurking behind his glasses.

"Let me just tell Jonathan where we're going."

SHERRY SPENT the next couple of hours trying to find some common ground with her son. But he didn't appear eager to do the same. He didn't have much use for horses or cows, or at least, that's what he said. He started to throw a rock at one of the cows and she had to stop him, explaining that it was wrong to mistreat animals.

"Oh, and I guess it's not mistreating them when you kill them and eat them?" he asked. "Anyway I wasn't gonna hit him hard. I just wanted to make him run."

"Still, throwing rocks isn't right."

He pouted and threw her hostile looks until they walked back to the house, where he spotted her red Firebird. "Whose car is that?"

"Mine." And she was quite proud of it. It wasn't new, but she babied it, and it shined with a recent wax job.

"Cool. Can I drive it?"

"In another three or four years."

"I can drive. Oleta lets me all the time. She sends me to the grocery store."

Good heavens! Something had to be done about this foster mother. "We better get back to the house. I really should get dinner started. Mr. Hardison's grandfather and his wife are coming home from their honeymoon anytime now, and I promised a special feast.''

''Like what?''

''Like pork chops and mashed potatoes and green beans and biscuits, and pie for dessert.''

''Oh.''

''You don't like pork chops?''

''I like pizza better.''

''Well, maybe tomorrow we can have pizza.''

''Yeah, right before you dump me off.''

''Chuck, much as I'd like to, I can't just keep you.''

''Why not?''

''Because there are laws about children and who can keep them.''

''But you're my mother.''

''Not legally. I signed papers—''

But he wasn't listening. He ran up to the house ahead of her, jerked open the front door and slammed it behind him.

If he'd given her a chance, she would have told him that she planned to look into things, like how she might become a permanent fixture in her son's life. She didn't think she'd be a good candidate as a foster mother, since she had a full-time job, but she really didn't know how these things worked.

One thing she knew for sure, though, was that she couldn't keep Chuck now. Her condo only had one bedroom, and she was sure no social agency would approve of making Chuck sleep on the floor or the sofa. She didn't know where Chuck would attend school, or who would take care of him while she was at work. She knew some twelve-year-olds could stay at home alone, but she felt Chuck was the type that needed adult supervision.

Clearly he hadn't been getting enough in his current living situation.

But these were all things that would need to be worked out, and they would take time. The last thing she wanted to do was make promises to Chuck that she wouldn't be able to keep. It seemed he'd had enough disappointments in his young life.

JONATHAN HEARD the front door slam. He left Kristin with her game and went to investigate, finding Chuck sitting on the sofa in the living room, arms folded, head down, kicking the coffee table.

"Excuse me, Chuck, but in this house we don't slam doors and kick furniture."

"Says who? You can't make me do anything."

"No, you're right, I can't. But usually when people invite you to stay in their house, you follow their rules. And if you can't, then you leave."

"I want to leave. I wish I'd never come here, but she won't let me leave. She said she would call the cops on me."

My, my. Sherry had a lot to learn when it came to parenting, though he supposed Chuck was a bit of a challenge. "And where's Sherry now?"

"Outside. She told me to get lost. She doesn't want me here, and neither do you. So why can't I just leave?" He gave the coffee table a particularly savage kick.

Jonathan couldn't help it. His temper rose. "If you don't stop kicking that table, you'll spend the rest of the evening in your room!"

"I don't even have a room!"

"I'll give you one! A damp, dark attic garret, equipped with chains."

Chuck's eyes widened and he stopped kicking the table. Jonathan realized the kid took him seriously. Maybe being locked in a damp garret wasn't beyond the realm of possibility in his world.

"Do I have to share it with anyone?" Chuck asked earnestly.

Regretting his hasty retort about the garret, Jonathan lowered his voice and smiled ruefully. "I was thinking you'd stay with my son, Sam. Ground floor, no chains, just bunk beds."

"Cool. Can I sleep on top?"

"You'll have to negotiate with Sam for that, but I expect he'll let you."

Chuck looked up at Jonathan with something approaching a smile. "Sherry didn't really say she would call the cops. I made that up."

Jonathan was relieved to hear that—and maybe a little disturbed that he was so willing to believe the lie.

Sherry came in the front door a few moments later, her face flushed. "Chuck, please don't run away from me like that."

"The cowboy here said I could spend the night in his kid's room," Chuck said triumphantly.

"I still need to speak to your social worker."

"Social worker?" Jonathan repeated.

"Chuck is in the foster care system," Sherry said. "His situation at home isn't the best. He ran away. I need to talk to someone."

Jonathan's face clouded with concern. "He can stay here as long as he needs to."

Sherry was overwhelmed by Jonathan's generosity. To just open his home to a strange child— "That's really nice of you."

"Yeah," Chuck said. Even her cynical child was impressed by the gesture.

Sherry decided she must have been wrong about Jonathan's coolness earlier. He'd just been surprised by Chuck's sudden arrival—as she was. Everything would be okay, now that Jonathan was in her camp.

Chapter Nine

"Chuck, do you have a social worker?" Sherry asked.

He nodded slowly.

"Do you know his or her name?"

"Carla somebody. I'm telling you, she'll want to come get me."

Jonathan took Chuck into the den to show him the TV so Sherry could talk privately on the phone. After a wild-goose chase through three automated phone systems, she finally got a live person who was able to put her in touch with Chuck's caseworker.

Carla was less than enthusiastic about Sherry's temporary custody of Chuck. "You can't just pass a kid around like he's a deck of cards!"

"That's why I'm calling. As soon as I realized Chuck was on his own, I contacted his foster mother. She gave me permission to keep Chuck overnight—"

"Does she know you? Personally, I mean?"

"Well, no. I offered to give her references, but—"

"For God's sake, what is Oleta thinking? Hell, I

know what she was thinking. One less can of beanie-weenies to open tonight.''

''I was a bit taken aback by Oleta's lack of concern,'' Sherry agreed.

''It's a good thing you called. I'll have to come get him, you know.''

''Can't I keep him just one night? I sort of promised him.''

''I'm afraid not.''

''Please, you can't just send him back to Oleta.''

''I wasn't going to do that. This isn't the first time we've had to question Oleta's parenting techniques.''

''Then where would Chuck go?''

''Probably to the children's home, till we can find him another placement.''

''You mean, like, an orphanage?'' Over her dead body.

''Well, it's not like *Oliver Twist*. It's a nice place.''

Sherry tried not to cry, but she couldn't help it. ''O-okay. Could he at least stay for dinner?''

Carla softened. ''I guess that would be okay.''

With a sense of foreboding, Sherry gave Carla directions to the ranch. She had all but promised Chuck he could spend the night. He would never trust her again. She felt this tremendous urge to grab her son and flee. But that would only be a short-term solution, and in the end she would get herself hauled off to jail with no chance of ever having a relationship with Chuck.

Or Jonathan.

She had to wonder what he thought of all this. He'd been kind to Chuck, but still rather reserved to her.

Was he appalled that she'd had a kid out of wedlock? She believed he was a fair-minded man once he understood the facts. It was getting him to listen to the facts before he jumped to conclusions that was the hard part.

She found Jonathan and the two children watching an animated video. Chuck looked bored and impatient. He glanced up when Sherry entered the room, his face reflecting both hope and another emotion, something like skepticism or doubt.

"Do I get to stay?" he asked, then almost cringed as he waited for her answer.

She shook her head, swallowing tears. "Carla is driving to Cottonwood to check things out. She said you don't have to go back to Oleta's, but she may not let you stay. I did my best. Jonathan, maybe when she gets here, you can talk to her and reassure her Chuck will be safe here."

"I'll do what I can."

SAM ARRIVED home from school, followed shortly by Pete and Sally's homecoming, preventing Jonathan from dwelling on the situation with Sherry. The newlyweds both glowed from their cruise. Pete's smile was bigger than Jonathan had ever seen before. But they were also clearly tired and hungry. They were pleased to find that Sherry was preparing a special meal for them.

"I'm tickled pink to have one more day away from the kitchen," Sally said, though she insisted on setting the table. "Well, well, well, who's this?"

Chuck lurked in the kitchen doorway, no doubt drawn by the scent of pork chops.

"This is my son, Chuck," Sherry said, as if she were testing out the phrase for the first time. "Chuck, this is Sally."

Chuck said nothing.

"I didn't realize you had children, Sherry," Sally said. "Chuck, would you like to help me fold napkins?"

Chuck darted out of the doorway, disappearing into another room.

"Sorry," Sherry said. "He's…shy."

"Shy?" Jonathan couldn't let that one slide.

"Well, all right, he's rude," Sherry admitted. "But there are special circumstances." She then did a creditable job of delicately explaining Chuck's background, and how he came to be here.

"Poor little mite," Sally said, clicking her tongue.

Sally took a special interest in Chuck during dinner, peppering him with questions about his upbringing, questions Jonathan was curious about, but that he wouldn't have had the nerve to ask. Chuck seemed resentful at first, but he warmed up to the older woman after a few minutes and forgot to be surly.

While this went on, Jonathan watched Sherry, whose gaze seldom left Chuck. He could only describe the expression on her face as…hungry. Clearly she had an interest in her son, but how deep did it go?

The social worker arrived just as Sherry finished clearing the table. Sherry rushed to greet the austere-looking gray-haired woman, whose dark eyes darted around the room, scanning everything, Jonathan presumed.

"Would you like some dessert?" Sherry asked. "We have pie and ice cream. And coffee."

"Chuck and I really should be getting back on the road," Carla said. "It's late."

"Couldn't we all sit and talk for a few minutes?" Sherry asked. She gave Jonathan a meaningful look. This was where he was supposed to reassure the social worker that the Hardison Ranch was wholesome, safe and nurturing.

"Well, all right," Carla agreed. "I can stay a while longer. And coffee would be lovely."

A few minutes later, all of the adults were seated in the living room discussing Chuck's fate.

"You won't find a better place for a kid to spend time," Sally offered. "He would have lots of supervision, space to play, nutritious food—"

"You all seem like lovely people," Carla interrupted with an apologetic smile. "I'm sure Chuck would be well off here. But I have rules to follow. Foster homes, even short-term ones, must meet a rigorous list of requirements. If you would like to apply as foster parents…" She looked uncertainly at Jonathan, then Sherry, not sure whom to address that comment to.

"But that takes a long time," Sherry objected. "Anyway, I'm not sure I'd qualify. I just can't bear the thought of Chuck going to an orphanage."

"It's just for a little while, till we find him another placement," Carla assured her. "It's a safe, secure place."

Those words echoed in Sherry's mind. *A safe, secure place where kids learn to respect themselves and others…in a natural setting, mixing fun with responsibilities…a rewarding learning experience a child will remember always…*

Where had she heard those phrases? Ah, she remembered. "Wait, I have a great idea. Wade's rodeo camp." She looked around the room to see how others were receiving her brainstorm. "Well?"

Sally smiled. She immediately saw the benefits of Sherry's idea, probably because she spent a lot of time at the camp. Jonathan, however, was frowning.

"Rodeo camp?" Carla asked, bewildered.

"My youngest grandson runs a camp for underprivileged city kids," Pete offered. "It's just down the road."

"There's a brochure around here somewhere," Sherry said. She jumped up from her chair and rifled through a stack of magazines on the bottom shelf of a bookcase, finally locating what she wanted. Triumphantly, she handed it to Carla, who looked with interest at the color photos of boys and girls riding and grooming and feeding livestock, competing in the ring, eating around a campfire.

"Wade is starting a new session this weekend, over Thanksgiving vacation," Sherry went on enthusiastically. "He has an amazing way with difficult kids." If ever there was a kid who needed some expert handling, it was Chuck. Sherry certainly didn't have a clue how to deal with him. Shoot, she had a hard enough time with Sam and Kristin, whom everyone else acknowledged as perfect children.

"I've heard of the Hardison Camp," Carla said, sounding impressed. "I've heard it's a wonderful place, too. But I understand there's an application process. And a waiting list. And costs involved."

"I'll cover the costs," Sherry said. "The camp is approved by the state. Wade has all kinds of certificates and licenses. Couldn't I just call him and ask him if there's room for one more? I'm sure he'll agree."

Carla looked into Sherry's hopeful eyes and caved in. "I guess it wouldn't hurt to call."

Sherry grabbed the phone and dialed Wade and Anne on the speed dial. In a matter of minutes, the deal was done. Wade had a last-minute cancellation that he hadn't filled yet, so Chuck was in.

"I'll go get him and tell him the good news," Sherry said excitedly.

She found Chuck again watching videos. "Haven't you heard?" she said. "TV will rot your brain."

Chuck looked at her sullenly.

"Don't give me that look. I've got good news."

"I can stay?" Chuck asked hopefully.

"Not exactly. But you don't have to go back to Dallas, at least not yet. You're going to camp."

"Camp?" Chuck looked disgusted. "No way. Not ever."

"It's rodeo camp, and it's just down the road."

"I said no!" he roared.

Sherry jumped. The other two children stared in disbelief.

Sherry stuck her chin out and adopted her sternest expression. "Do not raise your voice to me."

"You're not my mother."

The comment stung, more than any of the children could have guessed, but somehow Sherry swallowed back the hurt.

Carla appeared in the doorway. "Chuck, these people went to a lot of trouble on your behalf." Her voice was quiet but insistent. "Now get your things together. You're going to rodeo camp."

Carla obviously was another one of those people with a knack for exerting authority over children, because Chuck immediately acquiesced.

"All right, I'll go." Chuck nodded toward Sherry.

While Carla helped Chuck gather up his things, which he'd managed to spread all over the house, Sherry sought out Jonathan in the living room, where he sat on the sofa.

She sat down next to him. "Thank you, Jonathan, for helping out with this. I know Wade's camp is the best place for him." She threw her arms around Jonathan and kissed him on the cheek. But something didn't feel right about the embrace. Jonathan was stiff, and he made no move to return the hug.

She pulled back to look at him. "What's wrong?"

He shook his head. "Nothing."

"Bull corn, nothing. Do you think sending him to the rodeo camp is a bad idea?"

"Not a bad idea, no. Just not the best one."

"But why? I understand Wade really knows how to handle kids with problems. Clearly Chuck has some…issues."

"And whose fault is that?" The words were like a slap in the face. Before Sherry could retort, Jonathan spoke again. "No, I didn't mean that. I'm sure you didn't mean any harm to come to your son."

"I gave him up so he could have a better life than I could give him."

"How old were you?"

"Nineteen."

"Then you were hardly a child. You could have kept him. I know raising a child would have interfered with your plans, but—"

"It wasn't like that at all," Sherry said, her anger rising as she bounced to her feet. How dare he judge her? "You know nothing about what my life was like back then. You know nothing about being poor and not being able to see your choices clearly. You've always had this." She swept her arms to the sides, taking in the whole ranch. "I had nothing and I saw no future for myself, and I made the best decision I could at the time. As it turns out, it was the wrong decision and I've regretted it every day ever since. If I'd known what the future held for Chuck… I thought he would have nice parents and brothers and sisters and a dog."

Jonathan's face softened. "All right, so you made a mistake. We all do. But now your son has come back into your life, looking to make a connection. You've hardly exchanged three words with him."

"I've tried! In case you haven't noticed, he's not very receptive to my attempts at conversation. I think he truly dislikes me."

"He doesn't know you. And he won't get to know you if you send him off to camp."

"Is that what you think? That I'm foisting him off on someone else because I can't be bothered?"

"I just know that if I were you, I'd have taken him back to Dallas myself and immediately started whatever paperwork was necessary to keep my child."

"Well, you're not me. I'm trying to do what's best for Chuck."

"All Chuck needs is some firm and loving parenting. But you're not even going to try, are you? Maybe because he would cramp the cozy little life you've established for yourself?"

Sherry was shocked by the unfairness of the accusation. She wasn't abandoning Chuck so she could run back to Dallas and forget he existed. She very much wanted him to be a part of her world. But she was trying to proceed cautiously, for once in her life. She didn't want to screw this up.

She could tell by Jonathan's implacable expression that she could explain until she ran out of breath, and he wouldn't understand. He'd already made up his mind about her. She was a bad mother, an irresponsible parent, a career girl, a party girl who did not belong in a family situation. Today she had confirmed his worst suspicions about her.

Well, to hell with him. People had been judging her all her life based on scant or downright wrong information, starting with her parents. She didn't need Jonathan Hardison undermining the fragile self-confidence she'd only recently started to build.

She turned and headed for her bedroom.

"Where are you going?"

She whirled around. "To pack my bags, you opin-

ionated, pig-headed beast of a man. You don't have
a clue what you're talking about.''

"You're going back to Dallas? And leaving Chuck
here?''

"My plans are not your concern.''

She didn't cry. The white-hot anger inside her
burned away all the tears before they could reach her
eyes. She went straight to her room and started packing.

IT SHOULDN'T MATTER, Jonathan told himself as he
sank back into the couch. He'd been planning to end
things with Sherry anyway, right? Now she'd just
saved him the trouble.

But it did matter. He didn't want her to walk out
of his life forever, hating him. In the very short time
she'd been caring for him and his children, she'd gotten under his skin.

He thought about all the things she'd endured—all
the insults to her cooking, the make-over she'd gotten
from his well-meaning relatives, getting a frog thrown
at her, getting dunked in the bathtub…being seduced.
Putting up with Pete's fit of pique over his black-
polished ostrich boots.

He recalled how gently she'd cared for him when
all he did was growl at her.

None of that had driven her away. But after this
latest argument, she couldn't get away fast enough.

Maybe he was wrong about her. As generous as
she was, she must have had a very good reason for
giving up her child. But he just couldn't seem to get
past her reluctance to take responsibility for Chuck,

especially now. He couldn't help but feel sorry for the boy, who wasn't a particularly handsome or charming child. He would have a hard time of it unless someone took him in hand and straightened him out.

That person should be Sherry.

He went into his office to try to work, but he couldn't concentrate. A short time later, Sherry entered the room without knocking. "I'm taking Chuck to the rodeo camp, and I don't plan on returning to the ranch. So I'd appreciate it if you could write me out a check. You can mail it, if you want."

"You don't have to rush off."

"I told you I would leave as soon as possible, and that's what I'm doing. You obviously don't need my services anymore."

He felt the urge to argue. But that was just his libido talking. He still wanted her every time he looked at her. He couldn't help thinking about what she looked like underneath that ridiculous zebra sweater.

"I'll write the check now," he said.

"Thank you." She withdrew, leaving Jonathan with an empty feeling in the pit of his stomach, though he'd just eaten dinner.

He'd been too harsh with her. He knew that now. Years ago he'd driven his younger brother, Wade, away from the ranch with his pompous pronouncements on how Wade should conduct his life. And even years later when Wade had returned, seeking a new beginning, Jonathan had very nearly driven him away again by refusing to look at things from a different angle. His my-way-or-the-highway attitude had almost lost him a brother.

Was he doing the same thing now with Sherry? Maybe he should ask her to tell him the whole story of when she gave birth to Chuck.

He got out his personal checkbook and wrote Sherry a check for the agreed amount. When he went looking for her, however, she was dragging the last of her bags toward the front door.

He wanted to help, but with the crutches, he was pretty much useless in hauling anything around but himself. "Let me call Pete to get those bags," he said.

"No, thanks, this is the last of it."

"Where's Chuck? Shouldn't he be helping?"

"He's sitting in the car. He's mad at me."

Well, no wonder, Jonathan wanted to say, but he clamped his mouth shut, remembering his recent decision to speak less harshly about this situation. He knew how to be diplomatic, but for some reason, he found it difficult to curb his opinions around Sherry.

He held out the check. "I hate for you to leave like this. Couldn't we sit down and talk about it?"

"I have no interest in talking to you ever again," she said coldly, taking the check and stuffing it in her pocket. "I hope you and your high-and-mighty attitude enjoy the long, winter nights ahead—alone!" With that she whisked out of his house with her head held high, a queen dismissing an impudent subject. Jonathan felt properly put in his place.

And maybe he deserved it.

He could see it was no use trying to reason with her now. She was too angry. He'd give her some time to cool off, and try again in a day or two. He should just leave it alone, but he knew he wouldn't. Even now the compulsion to follow her was strong.

Any fool could see Sherry was the wrong woman for him. She wasn't the warm country girl with simple tastes that logic dictated would be best for him. Why couldn't he ever learn his lesson?

"I DON'T KNOW why you're bothering," Chuck said. "I'll just run away." He was slouched in the Firebird's passenger seat, arms folded, head down. Carla followed behind them in her own car, giving Sherry and Chuck time to say goodbye.

"If you do, you'll be picked up by the police and sent to juvenile detention, which is not a nice place, believe me. Is that what you want?" Sherry knew she should try to be more patient, more loving, more… something. But her fuse was short. Jonathan had seen to that.

"What would you know about juvie?" Chuck asked.

"Quite a bit, actually. I spent time there."

"Really?"

"Yes, really. I was hanging around with some guys who were smoking dope, and I got rounded up with the rest of them. My parents wouldn't bail me out, so I went to lock-up."

"Whoa," Chuck said with something that sounded like awe.

"You think it's cool having a mother with an arrest record?" It was sealed now because she'd only been fifteen, but still.

"Yeah, kind of."

Great. She'd been trying to scare him straight, and instead she'd become a role model. The wrong kind.

"Well, it's not cool. It sucks."

"I don't care if they arrest me," he said. "It'll happen sooner or later."

"Why do you say that?" she asked, alarmed by his attitude.

"'Cause that's what happens to kids like me."

"And just exactly what kind of kid are you?"

"One nobody wants. I'm not smart, I'm not good at sports, I'm fat and I'm ugly. The way I see it, a life of crime is all that's left."

Sherry's eyes burned. Dear God, what sort of crap had this child been listening to all his life? "I don't want to hear you say that ever again. Someone's been filling your head with a pack of lies."

"Oh, so I'm not fat? And I guess you've never seen me play basketball."

"Just because basketball's not your sport doesn't mean you wouldn't be good at something else. Like steer wrestling. It takes a big, husky guy to excel at that sport."

"Do they have that at this camp?" Chuck asked with his first spark of interest.

"Yes. I swear you'll have fun, Chuck, if you'll just give it a chance."

"I'd rather just go home with you."

"I'd like that, too, Chuck, but—"

"I know. It's complicated."

"I need some time to figure a few things out. But you're not getting rid of me." She turned her car into the driveway, where a sign proclaimed they'd arrived at the Hardison Rodeo Camp and Quarterhorse Farm. The long driveway was dark, but the big, old frame house that once belonged to Sally, Pete's wife, was lit up invitingly. A banner over the front porch said, "Welcome Cowboys & Cowgirls." In the thick woods behind the house, Sherry could make out the lights of the campers' cabins.

She had to practically drag Chuck out of the car and up to the front porch, where Anne greeted them, holding baby Olivia.

"This must be Chuck," she said with a big smile. "Come on in. Is this all your gear?" She looked down at Chuck's worn backpack.

"He only has one set of clothes," Carla, who'd joined them, said.

"Well, no problem, we have extra stuff you can wear, Chuck."

He gave her a surly look. "Hand-me-downs?"

"We call it 'share-wear' around here," Anne said cheerfully. "Wade will be back in a few minutes to get you settled. You'll be bunking with a boy named Belo and one of our counselors, Mark."

"Sounds enchanting," Chuck said with a sneer.

"Chuck, please don't be rude," Sherry said. "Everybody here is really nice, and they just want you to have fun."

"Yeah, that's what they told me about school." Chuck sat on the end of a sofa and did his best to ignore the three women.

Wade appeared a few minutes later to show Chuck his new quarters and go over the rules. Sherry tried to give Chuck a hug before he left, but he shied away from her touch and gave her a hateful look before reluctantly following Wade out the door. Carla went with him to check out the accommodations.

"Don't worry," Anne said as she set Olivia in a playpen. "A lot of the kids are angry when they arrive. It's usually not their choice to come here. They don't like being taken away from their friends and their familiar hangouts. But after a day or two, they chill out and start having fun."

Sherry stared at the door where Chuck had disappeared. "I hope you're right. I'm not sure that kid knows how to have fun."

"Then he'll learn. Do you have to rush off? I'm sure Jonathan's expecting you back. You've become pretty indispensable to him over the past few days. Or can you stay for a cup of coffee?"

Suddenly it all got to Sherry. To her embarrassment, she collapsed into noisy tears.

Anne didn't seem surprised or ill at ease over Sherry's display. She simply led her over to the sofa and sat beside her, rubbing her back, until the tears began to subside.

"All right, now tell me what Jonathan did."

"It's not just…Jon, it's…everything," Sherry said, struggling to bring her sobs under control. "This child I've dreamed about all these years suddenly appears, and he's nothing like I pictured. He doesn't like me, I'm terrible with him, I don't even like his name. Chuck Woods. It's like 'woodchuck' only backward. How could his parents do that to him?"

Anne put her arm around Sherry's shoulders. "This

has been a huge shock for you. You can't be expected to instantly adjust, and neither can Chuck. Now, what did Jonathan do?''

"Why are you so sure he did something?"

"Because I know my brother-in-law. He talks first and thinks later. He's a good man, and you couldn't ask for a more devoted father, but he thinks he knows how everyone should run their lives, and he doesn't hesitate to tell you.''

"That pretty much covers it," Sherry said. "He thinks I'm a horrible person for giving a child up for adoption, and now he thinks I'm trying to dodge responsibility again by dumping Chuck here. He didn't want to listen when I tried to explain.''

"Oh, he can be such a pompous—''

"No, don't say anything bad about him," Sherry said. "He's partly right. I *am* dodging responsibility. But I can't just suddenly claim a troubled, twelve-year-old boy and pretend I know what's best for him. I don't know anything about being a good parent.''

"None of us does when we start out," Anne said gently.

"So you think I'm doing the wrong thing, too?"

"No, of course not. Bringing Chuck here is the perfect solution—for now. But before the week is up, you'll need to decide what you want to do about him.''

"I want to be a part of his life.''

"His mother?''

"I don't know. Maybe I don't deserve to be his mother. I gave up that right, after all.''

"Oh, baloney.''

"What if I mess him up worse than he's already been messed up? I can't handle him. He doesn't mind me. He hardly listens to me."

"Which can be said about most twelve-year-olds. They're trying to assert their independence at that age. Don't take it so hard."

"I'm afraid of him, Anne. He's got so much anger inside him, and I'm afraid of how he'll express it."

"You just need to spend more time with him." Suddenly Anne's face lit up. "Hey, I know. Why don't you stay here?"

"And do what?"

Anne shrugged. "We need a cook. Sally usually handles that job, but she's probably not ready to come back to work. We were planning to muddle through without her."

"What would I have to do?" Sherry asked, warming to the idea. She was anxious to redeem herself and her cooking skills.

"It's easy. You have to buy the groceries, but the meals and shopping lists are already planned. Most of the meals are very simple—franks and beans, hamburgers, scrambled eggs, that sort of thing. If weather permits, we cook over the campfire at night, so all you have to do is a little prep work."

"I could do that."

"The pay is terrible."

"You don't have to pay me. I'll volunteer my services, if you'll just let me spend some time with Chuck."

Anne smiled. "Spending time with Chuck shouldn't be a problem. And of course we'll pay you." Then her smile faded. "Oh, but I forgot. There is one hitch. Thanksgiving."

"What about it?"

"We promise the kids a big, family-style Thanksgiving dinner with all the trimmings."

"I can do that."

"And we invite our families, too, so we can show them what healthy, functional families act like. And we'll be eating at the main ranch house."

That meant Jonathan. Sherry felt a flutter of apprehension, but she pushed it down. "I can handle it. I'm a good cook, despite what you saw that first night at the ranch, as long as I understand what's expected.

"Then you're hired."

Chapter Ten

The job of camp cook wasn't quite the walk in the park Anne had made it seem. Cooking for a dozen campers, three teenage counselors and the three adults meant lots of food. The preparations weren't challenging, just time-consuming.

After the first day, Sherry practically crawled to her small bedroom in the little foreman's house, which had been converted to a commercial kitchen. She was bone weary, and she worried she might never get the campfire-smoke smell out of her hair. She'd given up altogether on makeup or any sense of style when it came to her clothes.

Still, she'd gotten to spend some time with Chuck. She'd been careful not to monopolize his mealtime, which was an important part of socializing for a twelve-year-old. But she'd caught a few minutes here and there with him. He was still trying to hold on to a grudge against her for making him come to the camp. But any fool could see he was enjoying himself as he learned how to ride, rope and care for a horse. Sherry got to watch as he made his first solo ride around the practice ring. The triumphant smile on his face when he dismounted was like a gift from heaven.

After two days, she was gradually letting go of the idealized picture she'd held in her heart of "Brandon," replacing it with her real son, who was far more complex and interesting.

He was also far more challenging to handle than she'd ever imagined. He had a foul mouth and a tendency to bully some of the younger kids. Even his roughhouse play with the older kids was too violent, and Wade and the counselors had to keep a constant eye on him to prevent him from going too far.

He had quicksilver moods. One minute he would say something that was so darn sweet it would give Sherry a lump in her throat; the next he would turn angry and belligerent, threatening to throw a punch or run away. He reduced Sherry to tears of frustration more than once, and all the reassurances in the world from Anne and Wade wouldn't convince her that her child wouldn't end up in jail.

Then there was Jonathan.

Though she was too busy during the day to worry much about the frustrating rancher, at night her thoughts turned to him. She missed him. Although she couldn't overlook or dismiss his condemnation, she still missed the little things about him—like the way he looked all rumpled and drowsy in the morning; the strength in his hands as he opened a pickle jar for her; the way he'd pretended to enjoy her cooking even when she messed up.

She especially missed his gentleness with the children. She'd never seen a man so devoted to his kids.

His children were rambunctious and always into mischief, but he handled them with equal parts discipline and love, with an occasional indulgence thrown in.

She didn't imagine she would ever be that good a parent.

Several times she was tempted to call him. They'd both spoken in anger. Maybe now that they'd cooled off, they could talk more sensibly and she could make him understand....

But then she would think, no. She wasn't going to chase after Jonathan Hardison. No matter how strongly she was drawn to him, no matter how sexually compatible they were in bed, she was not going to pursue a relationship with someone to whom she was clearly mismatched. She needed a man who would accept her with her myriad faults and foibles, not try to mold her into his perfect little Stepford girlfriend.

But he didn't try to change you, she reminded herself. He'd liked the razzle-dazzle Sherry and had been unimpressed by her backward makeover. Then again, even as he'd been attracted, he'd not exactly approved of her. She suspected she was his guilty pleasure.

Well, no more. Sherry had made over more than just her makeup and hair. She was determined to be her own person, pleasing herself first, not only by the way she looked but the way she behaved. And to chase after Jonathan and try to make him forgive her when she'd done nothing so terribly wrong was not the sort of thing the new, improved Sherry would do.

So she didn't call him. But she did lie awake at night aching.

As THANKSGIVING LOOMED, Sherry's preparations for the big dinner grew feverish. The campers, staff and extended Hardison family numbered twenty-eight. Then there were the miscellaneous guests Sherry had invited, people she'd met in town who had no family in Cottonwood and no plans for Thanksgiving. Recalling all the holidays she'd spent alone, she'd asked Anne and Wade if she could add a few people to the guest list.

"You can use my paycheck for the extra groceries," she'd offered. She didn't need the money that badly, since Wade wasn't asking her to pay any part of Chuck's fees for attending the camp.

"Oh, don't be silly," Anne had scoffed. "You invite anybody you want, the more the merrier. The weather is supposed to be nice tomorrow, so we can spread out onto the patio."

At last count, Sherry figured she would have to feed at least thirty-five people. On Wednesday morning she made three trips to the grocery store as she, on different occasions, remembered items she'd forgotten.

As she returned from her third trip, Wade approached her car with a purposeful stride. She turned off the Firebird's engine and opened the door. "Don't tell me you need something else from the store."

"No. I guess Chuck's not with you, huh?"

Sherry's heart leaped into her throat. "He's missing?"

"One of the other kids teased him at breakfast. I probably should have stopped it, but I try to encourage the kids to work out conflicts on their own. Anyway, Chuck lost his temper. He threw a plateful of scrambled eggs at the other kid, then he took off. I thought he was just going back to his cabin, so I let him be. But when I checked, he was gone. I was hoping he was with you.''

''I haven't seen him. Oh, Wade, what if he's run away—I mean, really run away? He's done it before. He *hitchhiked* to get to the ranch.''

Wade pursed his lips. ''I'll call the sheriff. Can you think of where else he might have gone?''

Sherry shrugged helplessly. ''He might have gone back to the ranch. Sally was nice to him and Chuck took a liking to her.''

''Would you mind checking?''

''I'll call right now.''

Forgetting the groceries, Sherry ran inside the house and called up to the big house. She was relieved when Sally answered, rather than Jonathan, though at a time like this she was willing to put aside what now seemed like petty concerns.

''No, we haven't seen hide nor hair of Chuck,'' Sally said when Sherry explained the situation. ''But there are plenty of places around here for a kid to hide. We'll look around.''

''Thanks, Sally.''

Since Sherry would have been next to useless searching on foot and she certainly wasn't going to try riding a horse, she took off in her car, trying to think like an alienated twelve-year-old. Would he head for the main highway?

Deep down, Sherry didn't really think he would run back to Dallas. He would more likely look for someplace to hide for a while, to get his emotions under control.

As she approached the Hardison Ranch front gate, on impulse she turned in. Chuck had been looking for a home when he came here the first time. He'd liked the ranch house, and Sally, and he'd looked forward to playing on the computer. Sherry had a hunch this was where he'd headed.

As she passed the old red barn, she noticed one of the big double doors hanging ajar. A path where someone had recently walked through the tall grass was barely discernible.

Bingo. What better place could a kid find to hide?

Sherry pulled to the side of the driveway and parked. Her Firebird wasn't designed for venturing off-road, so she'd have to walk the rest of the way. There was a fence and a gate to pass through, but she didn't have a key.

As she closed her car door, she heard a soft rumble coming behind her. She turned, spotting the ranch's ATV heading toward her with Jonathan at the wheel. He pulled up next to her, and for a few moments all they could manage was to stare at each other.

She found she wasn't quite as angry with him as before.

"Jonathan, you should not be driving."

"My right leg is just fine." He cut the motor, reached behind him for his crutches and laboriously climbed out of the vehicle. He nodded toward the barn. "Looks like maybe you and I had the same idea. Cal and I searched all the other outbuildings. This was the last place I could think of to look."

"I'm not sure why I came this way," she admitted. "Maybe I just wanted an excuse to see you. I knew you'd know what to do about Chuck. Then I saw that the barn door was open slightly."

He gave her a crooked smile. "At least you're speaking to me."

"Yeah, well, Chuck's not the only one who gets into a snit now and then." She gave him an embarrassed smile, then turned away before she fell all over herself apologizing. Maybe she shouldn't have lost her temper, but Jonathan was the one who ought to be telling her he was sorry.

They headed for the barn. Sherry wanted to run, but she slowed her pace so Jonathan could keep up with her. She wanted to reassure herself that Chuck was here, that he hadn't hitched a ride with some psychotic serial killer, but she was also a little dubious about facing him alone.

When they reached the gate, Jonathan was stymied. He couldn't climb over it. Finally, with Sherry's help, he managed to squeeze through the barbwire fence, though he ended up sprawled in the grass after the complicated maneuver.

Sherry held out her hand. "Jeff should have put you in traction to keep you still and quiet."

He grasped her hand and let her help him up. "The leg is fine. I'm a fast healer."

She felt a ridiculous urge to tighten her hold on his hand and never let it go. And she did hold it for a bit longer than necessary, savoring the feel of his callused palm against her more tender one. Finally she forced herself to let go.

When they reached the entrance to the barn, they both stopped. Sherry hoped Jonathan would take the lead, go inside, find her son and deal with him. She felt woefully unprepared for the task. But he gestured for her to go ahead of him.

She slipped inside the dim, musty building. "Chuck?" The barn was filled to the rafters with hay. A kid could have a ball climbing around on the big round bales.

She got no answer. Maybe he wasn't here anymore, but he'd at least been here, Sherry was sure of it.

"Chuck? Please answer if you're here. I'm worried about you." She thought she heard a rustle, so she tried again, hoping she hadn't merely disturbed a rat. "I won't make you go back. I just want to know you're safe."

"Leave me alone."

Sherry breathed a huge sigh of relief as she glanced over at Jonathan. He gave her a thumbs-up.

Chuck's voice had come from the loft, where more hay bales were stored.

"Will you talk to him?" Sherry whispered to Jonathan. "I'm lost. I have no idea what to do now."

"You'll figure something out."

Panic welled up inside her chest. "Please, Jonathan, I'm scared I'll screw it up."

"No, you won't. Because you're coming from a place of caring. As long as he knows that, the actual words don't matter."

She took a deep breath. "Don't leave."

"I'm right here."

"Chuck?" she called. "Won't you come down from there, please?"

"I'm never coming down!" Chuck declared.

Sherry frowned. Then, from some source unknown to her, she suddenly knew what she had to do. She waited in silence.

"Did you hear me?" Chuck asked.

"Yes, I did. Okay, you don't have to come down," Sherry said. The only access to the loft was a rickety-looking ladder leaning against one wall. Gamely she kicked off her clogs and started climbing. Jonathan held the ladder for her. "Good luck," he whispered. "I'll wait for you outside."

When she was almost to the top, Chuck's face peered at her over the edge of the loft. "Hey, you said—"

"I said you didn't have to come down. I didn't promise I wasn't coming up."

Chuck sighed, exasperated. "It's a free country."

Gingerly she crawled onto the loft flooring. Her foot knocked against the ladder, almost toppling it, but Chuck reached out and snagged it just in time.

"Jeez, watch out. You'll get us both stuck up here."

"So you were planning to come down someday."

"Not until that cretin Jimmy Lutz is gone."

Sherry knew which one Jimmy Lutz was—the most abrasive kid at the camp, far more of a troublemaker than Chuck. He wasn't just a run-of-the-mill bully. He had a knack for finding a kid's weakness and exploiting it.

"I'm pretty sure Jimmy Lutz will be hanging around till Sunday. You'll get pretty hungry by then."

"I'm never eating again."

Now this was unusual. "So what did Jimmy do, anyway?"

"Nothing," Chuck mumbled.

"He must have done something."

Suddenly Chuck exploded. "He called me Chuckwagon Chuck! Because I eat too much! I hate my name, it's a stupid name! My mom and dad called me Charlie, but after they died, somehow it got changed to Chuck. I shouldn't of let 'em do it. I shouldn't of."

Sherry's heart ached for him. She realized this outburst wasn't just about one boy's teasing. It went to the very core of Chuck's identity and his memory of his parents.

He turned away, lying facedown in the hay. His shoulders shook, but he made no sound. Sherry settled cross-legged next to him and tentatively rubbed his back.

After a few minutes he seemed to relax.

"What would you rather be called?" she asked gently. "Charlie? Charles?" She liked both of those choices better than Chuck.

"Charlie's okay," he said, rolling over on his side to face her. He curled his arm under his head. "But it's too late to change it now. Isn't it?"

"It's never too late to change something about yourself you don't like." She'd already made one name adjustment, so what was another? "If you'd rather be Charlie, then start telling people that's what you want. I'll back you up.''

''Really?'' He almost smiled, but then he slumped back against the hay. ''I'm still fat.''

''Well, you're not exactly scrawny,'' she agreed. It would be silly to argue that he wasn't overweight. ''But you're at that age where not everything develops at the same time. You've got the weight now. Eventually you'll get the height to go with it. Your birth father was tall.''

''Really? Where's he at, anyway?''

Sherry shrugged. ''He was a real free spirit. Didn't want to be tied down with a family.'' She spent a few minutes telling Chuck—or rather, Charlie—about Don, all the nice things that had made her fall in love with him, leaving out most of the less pleasant aspects. This was the longest conversation she'd ever had with her son, and she was actually enjoying it.

Eventually she convinced him to return to camp and face Jimmy Lutz. ''Letting your temper get the best of you always makes things worse. That's exactly what Jimmy wanted. He was trying to get you in trouble.''

Charlie grinned as he held the ladder steady for Sherry to climb down. ''Yeah, but I bet he didn't want scrambled eggs in his hair.''

Outside the barn, they found Jonathan seated on a stump, waiting for them.

''What's he doing here?'' Charlie asked suspiciously.

''He was as worried about you as me,'' Sherry said. ''A lot of people were worried about you.''

"I guess I didn't think of that."

Jonathan ruffled Charlie's hair. "When Wade was a kid, he was always getting mad at somebody and hiding out in the barn. So you're in good company."

Sherry shot a grateful smile in Jonathan's direction. It was nice of him to try to make Charlie feel a little less foolish about his impulsive actions.

After much maneuvering around the barbed wire, they reached the car and the ATV. "Do you want to return to camp right away?" Jonathan asked. "You could have a cup of hot chocolate at my house first, if you want."

"I think I better get back to camp," Charlie said. "I'm probably in trouble."

"Wade won't be too hard on you," Jonathan said. "I'll talk to him."

Charlie flashed Jonathan a grateful smile, then climbed into the Firebird, leaving Sherry and Jonathan standing by the car, each waiting for the other to say something.

"Thank you," Sherry finally managed. "That was very nice. If you're not careful, you'll have me convinced you're really a kind and forgiving person."

"To everyone but you, it seems. Sherry, I know I went way overboard the night you left. I'm too sensitive where kids are concerned. You see, my ex-wife didn't really want Sam and Kristin."

"I'm sorry." That was all Sherry could think of to say.

Jonathan's faraway gaze said he was looking back in time. "Sometimes I think she got pregnant because all her friends were having kids and she felt left out.

But she paid the children very little attention. You know what her nickname was for Sam?''

''What?''

''Pest. What kind of message does that send a kid?''

Sherry thought of some of the nicknames her parents had labeled her with over the years and nodded.

''I could understand Rita leaving me. Maybe I wasn't the best husband. But rejecting the children our love created—that was something I couldn't begin to understand.''

''I'm not turning my back on Chuck.''

''I know that.''

''But I have to do things my way, at my own pace. I can't be an instant parent. I have to work up to it.''

Jonathan looked at her as if trying, really trying, to understand, though she wasn't sure he succeeded. ''Sherry? Why did you give him up? I have to know. Will you tell me the whole story?''

''I will. But right now I need to take Chuck back to camp.

''When you're ready.'' He leaned down and kissed her, a soft, sweet kiss that set the butterflies loose around her heart. Then he turned and maneuvered himself behind the wheel of the ATV.

THURSDAY MORNING dawned bright and clear, with just a nip of cold in the air. Sherry began loading up Wade's enormous SUV for her first trip to the main ranch house. She tried not to think about the fact that she would see Jonathan. She had enough distractions.

As she slammed the back door of the SUV, she

noticed a dark-haired figure heading toward her from the cabins, scuffing dirt as he walked. She soon realized it was Chuck—*Charlie*. He looked really cute in his borrowed Western wear. But she needed to do something about his broken glasses. She added that to her mental list of things she and Charlie would do once they were back in Dallas—she would take him to the optometrist.

"Hey, cookie," he greeted her sleepily, adopting the nickname Wade had coined for her. "I'm s'posed to help you load and unload stuff. It's my compensation for the scrambled egg thing."

Compensation was Wade's euphemism for punishment. He was big on the campers taking responsibility for their actions. If they broke something, they had to fix it. If they were mean to someone, they had to do something nice for that person. Sometimes they simply had to do an extra shift cleaning stalls. Occasionally they got stuck with kitchen duty, helping the cook peel potatoes or chop onions.

She hoped Charlie didn't view spending time with her as punishment. But getting up at sunrise to haul stuff around probably was. Still, it sounded as if Wade had let Charlie off easy.

"Well, you're a little late to help load the car," she said, "but you can ride with me to the big house and help me there."

"I won't miss the trail ride, will I?"

"I'll make sure you get back in time." The campers were taking a pleasure ride through the woods this morning, ending up at the ranch house for turkey dinner. "You like riding?"

"It's okay."

They climbed into the car, and Sherry started down the bumpy dirt drive toward the main road. "I talked to Carla yesterday. She's found you a new foster home. Get this—it's in Highland Park." Highland Park was one of the ritziest neighborhoods in Dallas.

Charlie made no response.

"You'll be their only foster child, and they don't have any children of their own. That probably means your own bedroom and bath."

"Yeah, sounds great," he said without much enthusiasm.

"You don't sound very pleased."

"Why should I? It won't last. I'll probably do something to screw it up and they'll send me back."

"Well, it seems to me that's entirely up to you."

"No, it's not," he said hotly. "You think I screw up on purpose?"

She thought about that. "Yes, I guess I did assume that when you misbehave, you do it on purpose."

"Sometimes," he admitted. "But sometimes I don't mean to. Like one time I was playing in this lady's car and I accidentally let off the parking break and the car rolled down the driveway and hit a tree."

"And what happened?"

"What do you think? I was out of there."

Sherry's heart went out to him. "Maybe this one will be better. You're older now, more mature. You have better judgment now."

She expected him to snort at that, but he didn't. He looked thoughtful.

"Also, you're going to have regular visitation with

me. One evening a week and one weekend a month, for sure, and maybe more if your foster parents allow it.'' The thought of having Charlie to herself for a whole weekend was intimidating, but exciting, too.

''That's what I'm worth to you, huh?''

Oh, hell, she should have known he would put a negative spin on her plans. ''I think we should take things slowly, that's all. I'm kind of like you—I screw up without meaning to. I get excited about things, then I do something on impulse and it turns out badly.''

That made her think of Jonathan. Ruthlessly she pushed all memories of their time together from her head. ''I don't want to screw up where you're concerned. I mean, what if I said, 'Okay, come live with me,' and then it turned out that you hated it? And then you started to hate me? I just couldn't stand it, Charlie, if you hated me.''

He studied her for several long moments. ''I used to hate you. Even when I came looking for you, I figured I'd hate you. I just wanted, you know, to see how you'd turned out. I figured you'd be a drug addict or something.''

Sherry knew she deserved that. She longed to ask him if he'd been pleasantly surprised by the real Sherry, but that would be begging for disappointment.

''I had a lot of crazy ideas about you, too, Charlie.''

It was the perfect moment for her to ask if he wanted to call her Mom, but she didn't. She was too afraid he would laugh or flatly refuse.

Sherry pulled the SUV around to the back door,

where Sally greeted them with smiles and a plate of homemade blueberry muffins. "My Lord, you have enough food there for a dozen family dinners!"

"It's mostly already cooked," Sherry assured her as they all unloaded the car. "All I have to do is reheat."

"Well, count me in, I'll help."

Anne and Allison showed up to help, too. Pete drove Charlie back to the camp along with Sam and Kristin, who wanted to join the trail ride.

"Do you notice anyone conspicuously absent?" Allison asked innocently as she folded a mountain of mismatched cloth napkins.

"Don't start," Sherry said, testing the temperature of one of the four turkeys she and Wade had smoked yesterday. "You think this bird's warmed all the way through?"

"Don't change the subject," Anne said. "He's clearly avoiding you, a sign of guilt."

"He's avoiding a kitchen full of women and cooking," Sherry corrected her friend.

"Actually, he's down at the barn," Sally said. She was working on a soup pot full of giblet gravy. "Jeff gave him permission to move around as long as he wasn't hurting, and Jon hasn't stopped since."

Sherry could picture that. The inactivity forced by Jonathan's injury had nearly driven him crazy. "I imagine he'll stay away as long as possible, given his attitude toward parties. I've gone and turned this simple family dinner into a massive shindig."

"I'm not sure you're right about that," Sally ventured. "He's mentioned about ten times this week that the house is too quiet. And your name has come up more than once, too."

"Oh, really?" Sherry wanted to kick herself for caring. But she was desperate for some scrap of evidence that Jonathan thought about her, that he missed her as much as she missed him.

"He must have told Pete and me three or four times about you inviting the choir to the house, and the Brownies, and the quilting ladies, and the square dancers—"

"They were cloggers," Sherry objected, warming to Sally's news like a flower warms in the spring sun.

"Well," Allison said, "he might have been complaining about you, but at least he's thinking about you."

"Oh, no, he wasn't complaining," Sally said. "He was singing your praises. He said he never thought being confined to a chair with a broken leg could be so much fun."

"Fun?" Sherry was bewildered. She'd never seen much evidence that Jonathan enjoyed her social gatherings.

"You made quite an impression on our Jonny," Sally said. "And I know you won't believe this, but he was running around with a dust cloth yesterday, making sure the house was in tip-top shape for Thanksgiving. So, no, I don't imagine he'll avoid the party."

And he didn't. Guests and family started arriving at noon, and Jonathan was there to greet them, get them a drink, invite them to watch football. The Dallas Cowboys pregame show was on TV in the den.

Sherry watched him with hungry eyes as he joked and laughed with everybody. Then he caught her staring. She looked away quickly, but not before she saw his knowing grin.

She'd never seen him in such a good mood. Did it have something to do with her? She wished she could find a way to get him alone. She was still thinking about that gentle kiss, which lingered in her mind even more vividly than their torrid lovemaking. And her promise to tell him about Charlie's birth.

The campers arrived just as the candied yams came out of the oven. Sherry was pleased with how the meal was turning out. She'd transformed herself into a pretty darn good camp cook.

During the meal itself, she hid in the kitchen. She felt naked, exposed, as if everyone at the table could clearly see her yearning for Jonathan. Anyway, there was so much to do, and she'd been sampling food all day, so she wasn't really hungry. But halfway through the meal, Allison and Anne invaded her refuge.

"Come on, Sherry, you need to sit down and eat."

"That's okay," she tried to protest. "I'm not really—no, c'mon, I don't need to—" But they weren't listening to her sputtering protests as they dragged her to the table.

There was exactly one empty chair, and it was right next to Jonathan.

Chapter Eleven

Jonathan smelled the conspiracy. His suspicions were confirmed when Allison and Anne took great pains to keep the chair next to Jonathan free and then all but dragged Sherry from the kitchen to sit next to him.

Not that he minded. He'd been keenly aware of Sherry from the moment she'd driven up in Wade's car, but he hadn't confronted her directly. He'd figured she had enough to worry about. But he'd caught sight of her off and on during the morning, and every time he'd glimpsed her, his chest squeezed a little tighter. He'd noticed the way her snug jeans outlined her cute bottom, of course, and how her sweater clung to her womanly curves, and the way her blond curls cascaded from her careless ponytail.

He'd also noticed her tennis shoes, and the fact that she wore little, if any, makeup. She was starting to look as comfortable in Cottonwood as Anne or Allison or any other woman he knew here.

Her lack of artifice didn't blunt his desire for her one iota.

Beyond her physical appearance, he noticed her manner with Chuck, or Charlie, as he was now being called for reasons unknown to Jonathan. She let him carry the turkeys in their flimsy aluminum baking pans, instructing him to support the bottom of each pan so it wouldn't collapse, then watching anxiously as he solemnly carried out the task.

Charlie asked her a lot of questions as he helped her in the kitchen, questions about food, the camp, horses and when she was little. Jonathan, pretending to listen to one of the "orphans" Sherry had invited, had instead shamelessly eavesdropped on the kitchen chatter as Sherry thoughtfully answered each and every one of the boy's questions as if it were the most important thing in the world.

He'd been wrong. He'd been so wrong to assume she didn't care about her child. Her caring shone from every gesture toward him, every look she gave him, every word she spoke to him. Jonathan still didn't truly understand why she didn't lay claim to Charlie, but perhaps he ought to try to see her point of view, instead of immediately assuming she was wrong and selfish.

Yes, he should definitely do that. But first he had to get close to her—in private. His emotions, which he usually kept quite well contained and controlled, were roiling around inside him like hungry piranhas, and he didn't want to put them on public display.

He passed one dish after another to her, earning a murmured thanks from her each time. As crowded as the table was, he couldn't help but brush elbows with her: their legs were only a couple of inches from touching under the tablecloth.

And he could smell her. Somehow, though the

scents of smoked turkey and ham and pecan pie and smoke from the fireplace mingled pleasantly throughout the house, Sherry's unique floral fragrance was still distinguishable.

"This is a great dinner, Sherry," he finally said. Talk about your lame compliments.

She looked at him, seemingly startled that he'd addressed her.

"You've cooked a wonderful meal, dear," Sally added as others agreed.

"Thank you, but I couldn't have done it without a lot of help. Wade spent all day yesterday smoking turkeys, and Anne put together the cornbread dressing. Oh, and wait till you see the beautiful pies Mrs. Schilling brought."

"You're too modest," Jonathan said. "You've done an incredible job. Take credit."

"Thank you," she said again without looking at him. Then, in a quieter voice, she said just to him, "I hope you don't mind all the extra people I invited. I know how you—"

"Sherry." He loved the sound of her name. "It's okay. I don't mind. If I wasn't willing to share my good fortune on Thanksgiving, I'd be a real...well, a turkey. But you were the one who was thoughtful enough to invite people who might otherwise have been lonely."

Her face turned rosy, but she said nothing.

"Is Chuck enjoying camp?" he said, trying to keep the lines of communication open. He knew he was treading on dangerous ground, but he figured she might want to talk about her son.

"Charlie," she corrected him. "Yes, I think he's enjoying it, although getting him to admit it is almost impossible. He's still trying to be a tough guy, though little by little he's opening up."

"What will you do when camp is over?"

It was the wrong question. She tensed. "I don't know."

He wanted to ask her to stay, but that would be selfish. He wouldn't require her to make a choice between him and her son, with whom she was obviously trying to establish a relationship. She couldn't do that if the kid was in Dallas and she was down here. But letting her walk out of his life would be awful damn hard.

She gave him an apologetic smile and stood, laying her napkin on the table. "Can I take anyone's plate?"

"You cooked, let someone else clean up," Pete said. "That's the rule around here."

"I'm being paid to do both," she said, not slowing down a bit.

"I'll help," Jonathan said. He managed to get out of his chair with a minimum of clumsiness, grab a couple of dishes off the table and hobble after her. He followed her into the kitchen.

She gave him a pleading look as she turned on the faucet. "You've spent far too much time on your feet. Just because Jeff gave you walking liberties doesn't mean you should overdo it. Now go sit down."

Instead he set the two dishes onto the counter and came up behind her, sliding his hands around her middle and resting his chin on her shoulder. "My apology is long overdue. Forgive me, Sherry."

She held her body stiff, refusing to yield to him. "It's not just a matter of forgiveness."

"You don't have to do it all at once. You can stay mad at me for a while, even yell at me if you want to. Just don't shut me out." He nuzzled her neck.

"Jonathan, this isn't the time or place." But she made no move to escape his embrace.

"There might not be another time or place. You're going back to Dallas in, what, three days?"

"I can't just—" Her objections were halted when Sally, Anne and Allison entered the kitchen.

"Okay, McCormick," Anne said to Sherry as Jonathan reluctantly released her. "You're officially barred from the kitchen for the rest of the day."

"But that's what I'm—"

"Yeah, yeah, that's what you're being paid your slave wages for. Get out. I mean it. Go watch football."

"I hate football."

"Then go outside and get some fresh air. Wade is getting ready to start a tour of the ranch. You've been here two weeks and you probably don't have a clue how things are run."

"It's not something I need to know." Sherry refused to relinquish her dish scrubber until Anne physically pried it out of her hand.

"I'm your boss, sort of," Anne said. "I don't care how you do it, but I'm ordering you to take the afternoon off and relax."

Finally Sherry flashed a grudging smile. "Yes, ma'am. I could use a walk." She left the kitchen through the back door, giving Jonathan a wistful look over her shoulder.

Allison gave Jonathan a pained expression. "Are you just going to stand there looking pathetic, or are you going to follow her?"

She practically sent Jonathan hurtling out the back door after Sherry.

Behind her, Sherry heard the distinctive cadence of Jonathan walking on his crutches. She slowed her pace so he could catch up with her.

"Anne's right," she said. "I don't know beans about this ranch. Want to give me a private tour?"

He grinned. "I thought you'd never ask."

Sherry had visions of finding an empty stall with big piles of sweet-smelling hay. She knew they still had things to work out if they wanted to make this relationship work. But she found it hard to think clearly when her hormones were in such an uproar, which they were, though Jonathan was simply walking beside her, not even touching her.

As they entered the barn she heard a frantic bleating coming from the other end. To her unpracticed ears, it sounded like a sheep. "Do you keep sheep at this ranch?"

Jonathan laughed. "It's a calf."

"Oh. It sounds unhappy."

"It is." Jonathan led her to a stall containing a rather pitiful-looking calf, bawling like his life was in jeopardy. He had numerous cuts all over his body and one particularly bad-looking leg. The cuts had been doctored with a purple medicine. All the purple spots and stripes might have been comical, if not for the injuries.

"Oh, poor thing," she murmured. She entered the stall and tried to pet it, thinking she might be able to calm it, but it was not interested in her caresses. Either it was in pain or hungry, possibly both.

She turned to look at Jonathan, who had a bemused expression on his face.

"What that calf wants," Jonathan said, "you ain't got."

"He's hungry, isn't he?" she said. "What does he eat?"

"Milk. But he'd prefer it from mom, not a bottle."

"Where's his mother?"

"She rejected him. He was a late calf, and the cow had a hard time of it. She knows winter's coming, and she thinks she can't possibly provide for herself and the calf, too. So she left him to die. He wandered off and got caught in some barbed wire. He's pretty worthless."

"Oh, how can you say that?" Sherry said indignantly, though she could barely hear herself over the calf's frantic bawling. "Can we feed him?"

"I was going to wait until the campers got here. They'd love the chance to bottle feed a calf. But it's way past his lunch time."

"Poor thing. Can't we at least feed him part of his milk?"

Jonathan nodded and disappeared, and Sherry continued to pet the calf and let it suck on her finger like a pacifier. He seemed to calm a bit. "Worthless," she muttered. "That's not very nice. It's not your fault you were born late and had a bad mother.'' Just like the circumstances of Charlie's birth weren't his fault, either. But he was the one paying.

A few minutes later Jonathan returned with what looked like a giant baby's bottle. He handed it to Sherry.

"How do I—"

"The calf knows what to do."

Sure enough, the moment the calf saw the bottle he grabbed the nipple and started sucking. But he drank only a few swallows before he spit out the nipple and turned away, losing interest.

"Is that all you want?" she asked.

"He's holding out for the real thing."

"Here now, baby, that's useless thinking. Mom is long gone, and you better make do with what's available." After a bit of coaxing, the calf started drinking again.

"Hey," Jonathan said, "you're doing pretty good. I think he likes you."

At least she was a good mother to something.

When the bottle was half-gone, the calf quit again.

"Maybe the kids can get him to take some more when they get here," Sherry said, putting the bottle aside and petting the calf. He seemed to like having the backs of his ears scratched. "Does he have a name?"

"We try real hard not to name an animal that'll just get sent to the slaughterhouse some day."

Sherry put her hands over the calf's ears. "Shh. Don't say that where he can hear." She removed her hands. "I think I'll call him Trouble. It sounds like he's always in it."

"Don't get too attached. I'll probably have to destroy him."

"Oh, my God, that's horrible. Why?"

"He's not exactly thriving. The ranch can only afford to put so many resources into one sickly calf before it becomes counterproductive."

"I'll take care of him," she offered on impulse.

Jonathan just rolled his eyes.

"Don't you worry, Trouble. I'll find a way to save you. Mean old Jonathan isn't going to toss you on the trash heap just because you're not perfect."

"I don't demand perfection," he said, a bit defensive.

All right, so she'd taken a potshot at him. Maybe that wasn't playing fair. "But you do like things your way," she countered.

Childish chatter and laughter drifted in, interrupting their conversation. Wade was here with the campers. Jonathan opened the stall door, and all the campers crowded just outside the stall to gape at poor Trouble.

"I think he's getting better, Daddy," Kristin said.

"He looks pretty sick to me," Jimmy Lutz said, stating the obvious. "Looks like his back leg's gonna fall off."

"What if he don't get no better?" asked one of the older kids.

"Yes, Jonathan," Sherry said, "why don't you tell the kids what happens to Trouble here if he doesn't shape up pretty fast."

"Life on a ranch can be pretty harsh sometimes,"

Jonathan said. "Weak ones have to be culled out of the herd. Otherwise, you start breeding weaknesses into the next generation."

"It's a good thing they don't do human beings that way," said one little girl Sherry had taken a special interest in. Tammy wore a brace on her leg to walk, but without the brace she was still able to ride a horse. Attending Wade's camp had given her the first opportunity to participate in a sport on an equal basis with other kids.

"What are you talking about?" Charlie said. "Human beings try all the time to cull out the weakest members of society. That's who *we* are. They call us 'troubled,' but that's a nice way of saying 'losers.' And that's why we'll all end up in jail."

"That's enough of *that* kind of talk," Sherry said sharply. "Every one of you has proved this week that you're strong and smart, and all of you have found something you're good at. Don't you *dare* let other people put labels on you."

The group got very quiet.

Sherry suddenly felt extremely self-conscious. All week she'd done nothing but dish up food and offer a friendly smile. Mild-mannered Cookie had never gotten on her soap box before.

"You tell 'em, Sherry," said Wade. "Y'all might not know this, but our camp cook, Sherry McCormick, used to be a 'troubled teenager' herself. But look at her now. She's a registered nurse, she owns her own condominium, and she drives that pretty red Firebird y'all have seen parked in the drive all week."

"Troubled, how?" someone asked.

Wade entered the stall and laid his hand on Sherry's shoulder. ''Sorry I put you on the spot like that. You don't have to talk about it if you don't want to, but the bits and pieces you've dropped to me and Anne over the past few days add up to an interesting story.''

Jonathan watched with undisguised curiosity.

''I don't mind talking about it,'' she said, though she did a little. Still, if even one of these kids could learn something from her mistakes and her triumphs, then it was worth a few moments of embarrassment.

So she told them everything—the trailer park she'd been raised in, her drunk, drugged-up parents, all the times she'd skipped school and been arrested for truancy, the drug bust, the time spent in juvenile hall, the year she'd spent drifting, working as a waitress and hoping some handsome, rich stranger would whisk her off and marry her, saving her from poverty.

''Believe it or not, getting pregnant is what saved me, though it almost killed me first. When my father found out I was having a baby, he beat me so severely I was in the hospital for a week. It's a miracle I didn't lose the baby. But it was in the hospital that I got to know a very special nurse. And it was there that I realized nursing was what I wanted to do, what I was put on this earth to do.''

She glanced over at Charlie, who was hanging back a bit after her chastisement.

''Still, it took me a while to pull it together. When I had my baby, my parents were going to throw me out on the street if I didn't give him up for adoption. I was really frightened by the thought of being homeless with a baby. So I did what they told me to do, even though it didn't feel right to me."

"And the baby was Chuck, right?" Sam asked.

"Charlie," several people corrected him.

"Oh, yeah, Charlie."

"Yes, that's right," Sherry continued. "Make no mistake, keeping the baby would have made life tougher for me. But I still could have become a nurse. Sometimes giving a baby up for adoption is the right thing to do. In my case, though, it wasn't." Her eyes filled with tears. "I'm really sorry I did that to you, Charlie. But we're starting over now, right?"

Charlie scuffed his boots against the barn's concrete floor. "Tryin' to, I guess."

JONATHAN LISTENED to Sherry's heartrending tale with a growing sense of guilt and shame. He'd gathered she wasn't raised by millionaire parents, but he'd had no idea the depths of her poverty or how far she'd come.

No wonder she'd wanted to give up her child. She'd had no reason to believe she could give Charlie any better life than she'd had.

"Well, that's enough about that," Sherry said, seeming embarrassed. "You didn't come down to the barn to hear a lecture. Wade, show us some horses and cows and stuff."

"You go ahead," Jonathan said to Sherry. "My leg is starting to ache." He gave what he hoped was a convincing wince and headed outside, where the ATV was parked.

Sherry followed him. "I told you you were trying to do too much."

He hid a smile. Sherry might be completely disgusted with him at this point, but she could not resist trying to help when someone or something was in pain.

Without a word she got into the four-wheeler with him. "You aren't really going to kill off that calf, are you? He's got such a sweet face. I named him Trouble."

"No one around here really has time to take care of him."

"How about the kids?"

"They'll be back in school next week."

"Then I'll take care of him."

"Oh, really? Are you going to take him back to Dallas in your Firebird? Keep him in your condo?"

"I'll think of something. Maybe you could donate him to a petting zoo."

"Do you know what happens to petting zoo animals when they get too big?"

"Let's just change the subject. Do you want to take some aspirin or Tylenol for your leg?"

"No. It doesn't really hurt. I just wanted to get away from the crowd."

When they arrived back at the house, Sherry solicitously helped him out of the vehicle. Though he was perfectly capable of getting along by himself, he let her assist him. He wanted any excuse to remain close to her.

"About what you said back at the barn..."

"Don't make a big deal about it. I told that story

for the kids' benefit, not so people would feel sorry for me or make allowances.''

''I'm not feeling sorry for you, I admire you. You've come a long way.''

She looked at him for a long time. ''I'd be in a very different place if I'd kept Charlie. Maybe you're right. Maybe it was a selfish decision.''

''Well now is a hell of a time to start listening to me when I've already admitted I was wrong.''

''Maybe there's no right and wrong, Jonathan. Did you ever think about that?''

He sank back onto the seat of the ATV. What in tarnation did she mean, no right and wrong? Of course there was right and wrong. It wasn't very often he admitted to being the latter. Why didn't she enjoy it more?

Well, at least she was talking to him. If only he could remember not to shoot off his mouth before his brain was engaged, he might avoid alienating her again.

Sherry started for the back door, then stopped and went around to the front instead. Jonathan saw what had caught her attention. A pint-sized pony was calmly munching on flowers in the garden.

''Oh, dear!'' she said, sounding distressed. ''No. Shoo! Sally's going to be very unhappy with you, horsey, if you don't get out of these flowers.'' She waved her hands ineffectually at the horse.

Jonathan joined her in the front yard. ''That's Misty, Kristin's pony. I've never known a more willful animal.''

''Make her get out of the flowers.''

"Just pick up her lead rope and drag her back to the other horses."

She hesitated, then picked up the rope. When the pony stopped chewing and gave Sherry a malevolent look, Sherry dropped the rope and took a step backward.

"Are you afraid of horses?" Jonathan asked.

"Absolutely. They're pretty, but they're big and I understand they bite."

"Come here." Abandoning Misty, they walked over to where some of the other horses were tethered.

Sherry crossed her arms. "I'd like to know who's going to clean up all this horse poop."

"The campers will do it." He paused before a big bay horse. "This is Traveler, and he never bites. He took Wade ninety percent of the way to his calf-roping championship. Hurt his leg the day before the finals in Kansas City. Wade almost lost the whole ball of wax."

"But he didn't. I've seen that gold buckle."

"He rode another horse in the finals, a mare named Cimmaron."

"Oh, the pretty black one," Sherry said, pointing to where the flashy black horse was grazing. "Don't tell me *she* doesn't bite. I know better."

Jonathan chuckled. "Cimmy is a certifiably psychotic horse, all right. I thought Wade was crazy when he asked me to drive her up to Kansas City so he could compete with her. But it was his only chance to salvage the championship, so I did."

It had also been his last chance to salvage his relationship with his brother. Anne, who had just reconciled with him herself, had played a hand in getting Jon and Wade to let go of the past and truly be brothers again.

"And he won," Sherry said. "Against all odds."

"Sometimes you have to ignore the odds and take a risk."

Sherry might be blond but she certainly wasn't dumb. She knew he wasn't just talking about Wade and his horse.

When she didn't respond to his opening gambit, he nodded toward Traveler. "Hop on."

"What? You want *me* to climb on the back of that huge thing? Don't think so."

"Chicken. This is the gentlest horse on the ranch."

Sherry just couldn't walk away from the challenge. "All right, I'll climb on his back. I'm not afraid." After several clumsy attempts to mount, Sherry finally managed to get her butt in the saddle. She held on to the saddle horn for dear life.

"Okay, I did it. Now help me down."

Jonathan untethered the horse and looped the knotted reins over Traveler's head, handing them to Sherry. "Walk around the yard with him."

"I can't do that!" But she did. Jonathan gave the horse a friendly slap on the rear to get him started. He plodded around the front yard, somehow knowing exactly what Jonathan wanted from him.

"Okay, this is scary." Sherry's voice quaked. "How do I get him to stop?"

"Very, very gently pull on the reins. Don't yank."

Sherry did as instructed. Traveler obligingly came to a halt and stood patiently.

"That's enough for my first riding lesson," Sherry said. "Now get me down."

Her dismount was even worse than when she'd climbed on. Jonathan tried to help, but she ended up falling on him. They both tumbled onto the grass.

"Oh, hell," Sherry said, her first concern for Jonathan. "Did I hurt you?"

He laughed. "I wish someone had been taking a video. That was about the clumsiest thing I ever saw."

"Sure, make fun of the city girl." But soon she was laughing, too. When they couldn't laugh anymore, Sherry helped Jonathan to his feet. But she made no move to go inside, though he knew she was cold in her thin sweater. Instead she petted Traveler.

Jonathan knew it was time to say what needed to be said between them. He might not have another opportunity.

"So do I get a second chance? Or maybe I'm on my third or fourth chance by now."

She sighed. "Getting involved with you would be a crazy thing for me to do."

"We're already involved."

She shook her head. "We almost were. But then I saw what I would be getting into. Jonathan, I'm one of those people who likes to please others. I'd spend my whole life turning myself inside out to please you. When I succeeded, you would lavish praise and attention on me. But when I failed to meet your expectations, I would suffer the consequences."

She continued to pet the horse, having accidentally found one of the places he loved to be scratched, under his jaw. All the while she was casually annihilating Jonathan's character.

"You said you didn't care about my clothes or my hair," she continued, "and I was very encouraged by that. I thought that at last I'd found a man who could accept me as I am. But you haven't."

"But that's not—I mean—"

"Face it, Jonathan. You wanted me to do all the changing, make all the effort."

"But I've admitted I was wrong."

"This time. But what about tomorrow, when I make another decision you don't agree with?"

"I have to speak up when I think someone is making a mistake."

She shook her head. "You're not getting it. A mistake by whose standards? Yours! You may think I'm a tough cookie, Jonathan. I try to appear that way. But I'm not. I've been kicked around way too much for one lifetime. People have been passing judgment on me from the time I could walk. I'm not up to it anymore. I don't want to have to defend my decisions, about Charlie or anything else. I need to just take care of me and worry about my son. I don't need to worry about pleasing anyone else."

"Are you saying there's no hope?"

She nodded miserably.

"God, Sherry, you can't mean that. I know I upset you, but I also know you care for me." She couldn't have made love to him the way she had, with her whole body and soul, if she didn't.

"I do. I won't deny it. I might even…love you. But I can't be with you right now."

This time he let her walk away. He didn't know what else to do. Did she really think he meant to tear her down with criticism? He hadn't intended that. He hadn't wanted to hurt her. He'd just been so stunned by her behavior toward Charlie. He'd wanted to shake her up, make her see reason. He knew he had a bad habit of telling people their business, but his motives were pure. He only wanted them to make the right decisions.

If Sherry made the wrong decision with Charlie, she would regret it forever.

He looked longingly at Traveler, wishing he could just hop on the horse and ride, gallop across some field at full tilt and escape the desolation that was creeping up on him at the thought of a future without Sherry.

Chapter Twelve

It felt good to finally get off his feet. Jonathan claimed his favorite recliner in the den and watched the end of the Cowboys game, letting a wild array of people—Sherry's strays—distract him from his dark thoughts. Many of them were people he saw all the time: Clem from the grocery store; Esther, who cleaned for him; an elderly widower from church. He'd never taken the time to get to know them before.

Sherry had made him realize what a cantankerous recluse he was turning into. Maybe she'd saved him before he became one of those grumpy old men children run from and women cross the street to avoid.

After the game, a disheartening defeat for the 'Boys, the house gradually emptied. Wade and the campers left, taking Sam and Kristin and all the horses with them. Finally it was just family left—Pete and Sally, Jeff and Allison, Edward, Anne and Olivia.

And Sherry. Anne had insisted she take the evening off, that the campers could fend for themselves for one night. Then, still in matchmaking mode, Anne had deliberately stranded Sherry at the ranch house.

Someone had already taken the SUV back to the camp, loaded with leftovers.

Sherry stayed away from Jonathan, and he tried not to crowd her. She was thinking about him—stealing covert glances at him when she thought he wouldn't notice. He would give her time to think things through and come to the logical conclusion that they shouldn't give up on having a relationship.

At about eight o'clock, people started getting hungry again. Naturally, Sherry rushed to make turkey sandwiches for everyone. She dragged dishes out of the refrigerator and put on a buffet almost as lavish as the Thanksgiving meal had been.

"She's really quite the little hostess, isn't she," Edward whispered to Jonathan. "I was all wrong about her. I thought she'd be a wash."

"She's got a high gloss, but it comes off pretty easy," Jonathan said, feeling almost proud of her, certainly proprietary.

"You talking about Sherry?" Allison asked, scooting her chair closer to join the conversation. "I told you she was good people. Y'all didn't believe me. So, Jonathan, have you talked her into moving to Cottonwood?"

"Good God, Allie, no."

"You don't want her to?"

Of course he wanted her to. It wasn't that easy. "She's got a job and a condo in Dallas, not to mention a son."

"She could have all those things here, too," Allison said. "Except maybe the condo. But she could buy a big house here for the same price she paid for a teensy one-bedroom in Dallas.''

"You know, our nurse, Molly, is quitting next month," said Jeff, who'd been eavesdropping. "Her husband's taking a job in Atlanta. We haven't found a qualified replacement. Sherry could have that job in a heartbeat.''

"But what about the boy?" Jonathan asked. "His foster home is in Dallas.''

"Has she thought about adopting him?" Anne asked. "I'd do the legal part for free and I've actually got some experience in that area. I did an adoption for a woman over in Rutledge. She adopted her biological daughter that she'd given up at birth, so I know it can be done.''

Jonathan's heart beat faster as the possibilities were rolled out before him...to have Sherry here, in Cottonwood, permanently. She and Charlie could spend weekends with him at the ranch. Sherry and Sally could swap recipes and do friendly battle over the kitchen. Sherry could mother his kids along with her own child.

It would be perfect, if only he could make her see that.

Sherry walked into the dining room carrying a pitcher of iced tea and a bowl of fruit salad. "What are you talking about, huddled up over there like you're conspiring about something?" She asked the question good-naturedly, but when the room went silent, she looked perplexed.

"Actually," Allison said, "we're plotting your future. Anne's just had the most wonderful idea. She said she'll do the legal work so that you can adopt Charlie.''

"I was saying I just did a similar adoption," Anne added, "and it was pretty easy. We would just have to show that you're settled and stable now. Of course there are background checks—"

"Oh, that won't be a problem for Sherry," Allison said with a dismissive wave of her hand. "She's a total straight arrow now, right, Sherry?"

Sherry nodded but said nothing as she set down the pitcher and bowl, then sank into the nearest chair, looking as if her legs wouldn't hold her up any longer.

"We've got a job available for you, too, a real nurse's job," Jeff said. "I'm sure it doesn't pay what the plastic surgeon was going to pay you, but the cost of living in Cottonwood is really low."

"Oh, and I know the perfect house for you!" Anne said. "It's a little Victorian, just off the square. It went on the market only last week, and Mom says it's priced way too low."

"Um, gee, I don't know…." Sherry said.

"Well, if you don't like Victorian, there are lots of other choices," Allison said blithely. But Jonathan knew the style of the house wasn't the problem. He was the problem.

Pete, who'd been pretty quiet during this discussion, spoke up. "Y'all might want to give the girl a chance to breathe. You expect her to make a decision about her whole life based on some dinner-table chit-chat?"

"Yes, thank you, Pete," Sherry said, looking relieved. "You all have given me a lot to think about."

"But the job opening won't last forever," Allison pointed out, "and neither will the house."

"And the adoption red tape takes time," Anne said. "You'll want to get started as quickly as possible."

"I'm not—" Sherry stumbled. "That is—"

"What is it, sweetie?" Sally asked, her gray eyes filled with concern.

"This is moving much too fast for me." She tried to smile, but it didn't come off. "I'm not ready to adopt Charlie and I can't move to Cottonwood. Much as I love the town and everyone here, it's just impossible."

"But why?" Allison asked innocently. "It's everything you want all rolled into one happy nutshell."

Anne laid a hand on Allison's arm and subtly shook her head to forestall any further argument. But the question was already out.

It got so quiet at the table that Jonathan could hear himself breathing. Or maybe it was just that he was breathing extrahard. Sherry stared at all of them. She opened her mouth to speak, but no words came out. Then she pushed away from the table and calmly left the room. Moments later the front door opened and closed.

Everyone at the table let out the breath they'd been collectively holding.

Anne folded her arms.

"Thank you all so very much," Jonathan said.

Jeff toyed with his pecan pie. "I was trying to help."

"You all agreed with me," Allison said, "It was a great plan!"

Pete cleared his throat. "Any fool could see we were upsetting her by rearranging her whole life. Maybe adopting the kid and moving here to the sticks is exactly what she wants, what would be best for her. But it's a decision she has to make for herself. Give Jon some credit. He knew this wasn't the time to rush her."

Sally hit Pete with a napkin. "Since when did you know anything about rushing? It took you twenty years to propose to me."

"Maybe I better go after her," Jonathan said.

"Let her stew a bit," Edward said. "I don't think she put on a jacket, so she'll be back before too long."

But Sherry didn't come back anything near soon. An hour passed and she still hadn't returned. The others were playing some card game around the dining room table, but Jonathan couldn't focus on the spots and had quit after the first hand. He was starting to worry, though he knew the chances of her getting eaten by a mountain lion or kidnapped by a crazed serial killer were pretty remote.

Still, she could have gotten kicked by a cow or fallen into a gopher hole and turned her ankle.

"I'm going to look for her," he finally declared, getting up from the table.

"Don't be ridiculous," Jeff said, laying down his

hand of cards. "You won't get far with that gimp leg. I'll go look for her."

"I'll help," Allison offered. "It's my fault she was upset. I don't know what I was thinking, pushing her like that."

Anne, who'd been watching and listening intently, stood up. "Jonathan and I can take the four-wheeler and search," she said.

Glad to be finally taking action, Jonathan put on his jacket and helped Anne with hers. Pete and Sally agreed to stay and watch Olivia, but everyone else was going to look for Sherry.

Anne started up the ATV's engine and slowly eased the vehicle down the driveway. They both scanned the pastures on either side for signs of Sherry.

"I really am sorry," Allison said. "I guess we should have minded our own business. But I think you and Sherry make a great couple."

"She doesn't see it that way."

"Why not? What's not to love about you?"

He was beginning to wonder.

"I'm doing it again," Allison said. "I'll keep my mouth shut."

"Let's just find Sherry."

"Maybe she walked back to the camp."

"It's a long walk in the dark."

"If she was mad enough and determined enough, she could do it. Let's head in that direction."

"Okay." Anne took the ATV out onto the main road. Minutes later they were driving up Wade's driveway. Sherry's Firebird was still parked near the house, which was somewhat reassuring. At least she hadn't gone back to Dallas.

The glow of a campfire was clearly visible through the trees. "Wade was planning for the kids to camp out under the stars tonight, if the weather cooperated."

They drove the ATV to the edge of the trees, then got out and walked to the clearing where the campfire roared cheerfully. Jonathan scanned the kids, huddled in their sleeping bags, hoping to catch sight of Sherry. But she wasn't there. His hopes crashed.

Wade put down the book of horror stories he'd been reading and smiled. "Haven't you all had enough of us? Or did you come for more abuse?"

"Sherry's missing," Jonathan said quietly, so as not to announce the fact to all of the kids. "I was hoping she'd come here."

Wade's smile faded. "She hasn't showed up here. What do you mean, missing? Did she run away from home? Jeez, bro, what did you do this time?"

"All right, that's enough out of you," Anne scolded, stepping between the two brothers before they could come to blows. Although they'd ended their feud more than a year ago, each of them still had the ability to rile the other one almost without effort. "We need to find Sherry."

"Did you check up at the house?" Wade asked. "I left the door unlocked."

"We'll check," Jonathan said, "but the house looked dark." That was when he realized that someone was listening in on the conversation. He must have crept up quietly when he heard Sherry's name mentioned.

"Did you say my mom's missing?" Charlie asked, his voice thick.

Jonathan hadn't thought about how this incident might affect the boy. That was the first time he'd ever heard Charlie refer to Sherry as his mother.

"It's probably nothing to worry about," Anne said quickly. "She got mad at us and went for a walk. I'm sure she'll come home when she's cooled down, but we want to find her so we can apologize."

"I bet I know where she is," Charlie said.

"You do? Where?" Jonathan asked, though he doubted one twelve-year-old boy could outguess a handful of adults.

"The same place I hid out when I ran away."

"Oh, hell, why didn't I think of that?" Jonathan said. "The old barn."

"I'm coming with you," Charlie declared, abandoning his sleeping bag and pulling on his boots. Jonathan was reluctant to deny him, though getting all three of them into the ATV would be a tight squeeze.

"Cool, I've always wanted one of these," Charlie said when he saw the four-wheeler. "Can I drive?"

"No," Anne and Jonathan said together. Then Jonathan added, "I'll let you drive it in the daylight, in the pasture."

"Cool."

As they neared the old barn, Anne cut across an expanse of dried grass between the driveway and the aging wood structure silhouetted in the moonlight. They stopped to open a gate and shut it, a task Charlie performed as if he'd done it all his life. He looked different from when he'd arrived, Jonathan noticed. He stood taller and moved with more confidence. His complexion had some color. Sending him to Wade's camp had probably been the best thing for him. Jonathan wasn't sure why he hadn't been more enthusiastic about it.

Anne pulled up in front of the weathered building and cut the engine.

"I want to go in first," Charlie said. "I want to find her."

"We don't even know that's where she is," Anne said.

"She's there," Charlie said with certainty. "I want to find her."

That was fine with Jonathan. He had no idea what he'd say to Sherry when he saw her, anyway. He handed Charlie a flashlight.

SHERRY HAD DOZED OFF when voices awakened her. Thank God, someone had found her. Though she'd covered herself with hay from the loft where she'd come to sulk, she was still freezing. The old barn was hardly windproof.

Then she wondered who had come looking for her. *Not Jonathan,* she hoped. Surely he wouldn't hike around with a search party.

The old door creaked open, and she saw a flashlight beam enter. She couldn't see who was holding it.

"I'm up here," she called, waving.

The flashlight hit her in the face. "Sherry? That you?"

"Charlie?" Of all people, she wasn't expecting him to find her. When a grown woman ran away from home, it was embarrassing for her twelve-year-old son to track her down.

"Hah. I knew I was right, I just knew it." He came closer, averting the flashlight beam from her eyes. "What are you doing up there? Everybody's worried about you."

"Look." She pointed at the ladder, which lay on the dirt floor of the barn. "It slipped when I came up here. I've been stuck."

To her surprise Charlie didn't laugh at her clumsiness. "I'll get you down," he said gallantly. He laid the flashlight aside, picked up the ladder and leaned it up against the floor of the loft. But instead of standing aside so she could climb down, he started climbing up.

"If you're not careful, two of us will be stuck up here," she warned.

"*I* know how to climb a ladder." In moments he was beside her. "I thought you might need someone to help you down. Girls aren't very good at those kinds of things."

"Charlie Woods, don't ever let me hear a sexist comment like that from your mouth." But she couldn't muster much censure in her voice. She was really glad to see him.

Neither of them made much of a move to descend the ladder. "Could I talk to you?" he asked tentatively.

"Of course. You can always talk to me. Anytime, about anything."

"All that stuff you said at the big barn earlier today, when we were feeding the calf. Is it all true? About your father beating you up and stuff? Or was that just a story, to be inspiring or something?"

"No, it's all true. I hope it wasn't embarrassing for you."

"Oh, hell—heck, no. Everybody thought you were pretty cool. And that made me cool. Well, a little bit, anyway. They were all asking me if I was going to live with you."

"Would you like that?"

"Only if you wanted me," he said softly.

Sherry couldn't help it—she threw her arms around him. "Oh, honey, oh, baby, I do want you. More than anything in the world. But—" But what? "I'm afraid. That's what it is."

"Afraid of me?"

"Afraid I'll be a terrible mother. I don't have any experience at it, remember? Most mothers get to start with a little baby and little babies are easy, they just cry and drink milk and sleep and need a diaper change. Then they slowly start turning into big kids, so the mother gets to practice a little at a time. I haven't gotten that chance."

"Well, you *act* like a mom."

"I do?" She had a hard time believing that.

"Maybe not at first, but you do now. You yelled at me a bunch today."

"I did not yell!"

"Yeah, you did. You know, 'Don't stick your head in the oven, you'll gas yourself.' 'Be careful with that knife, you'll cut off your finger.' 'I don't want to hear that word out of your mouth ever again.'"

All right, so he did a pretty good imitation of her. "That's not yelling," she objected. "That's—"

"That's being a mom. You're learning real fast."

Holy cow. Maybe he was right. Maybe she wouldn't be June Cleaver every day, but she was smart and determined and compassionate, and she had a lot of love to give. Surely she was entitled to try.

She was being given a second chance with her baby. And she was perilously close to blowing it. Jonathan had been right, about that, anyway.

"You know what, Charlie? Anne offered to help me apply to adopt you, and I think I'll let her. If you want me to. I mean, you'll be giving up a home in Highland Park."

"Yeah, and some nice lady and her husband who think they're real noble 'cause they're taking in some poor kid. I'd rather have a real mom."

Sherry hugged him again, and this time he let her. He even hugged her back, and it felt like he meant it.

Eventually Charlie extricated himself from her smothering, seeming a little embarrassed by it. "Yeah, okay. Let's not get too sloppy here. Anyway, your boyfriend is waiting outside."

"Jonathan?"

"Right here," said a voice from below. "I'm right here, and I'm not going anywhere."

"That's my cue. I'm out of here." Charlie scampered down the ladder faster than Sherry would have thought possible, given his size. "She's all yours, dude," he said to Jonathan.

"I kind of doubt that," Jonathan said as Charlie left the barn. Then he looked up at the loft. Sherry could barely make out his face in the glow from the flashlight, which sat on the ground with its beam facing up. "Are you coming down, or do I have to come up and get you?"

She visualized him scaling the ladder with his broken leg and realized he'd probably try. "I'm coming down."

He held the ladder steady as she descended—right into his arms. He grabbed on to her and wouldn't let her escape. "Whoa. Where are you going?"

She struggled only a moment longer before relaxing against him.

"There, that's better."

"This is a very dangerous place for me to be," she said.

"Why? I don't want to hurt you. You have to believe that."

"I do. I know you mean well." She turned to face him, looping her arms around his neck and tucking her head under his chin. "But if I let you hold me like this, I'll lose my grip on reality. Then I'll start spinning fantasies that could never come true."

"What kind of fantasies?"

"You know, fairy-tale stuff. Happily ever after."

"Is that so far-fetched?"

"Fairy-tale princesses are always perfect."

"I thought we determined I'm not a perfectionist."

"Oh, Jonathan, I'm not just imperfect, I'm a mess.

I'm flawed. I'm impulsive, and sometimes I'm selfish, and sometimes I'm a coward.''

"I like you the way you are."

"You say that now, but—"

"I love you, Sherry. I promise I won't rush you again, and I'll tell my family to leave you alone. You have a lot on your plate, and I understand completely why you don't want to make any impulsive, life-altering decisions. I can wait."

Her heart had stopped beating when he said the word "love." No man had ever professed to love her before. It was one of those pesky fantasies she'd carried around with her for what seemed like forever—a handsome, good-hearted man holding her dear, thinking she hung the stars, putting her in the center of his universe.

But words were cheap; actions took strength of character. Jonathan had shown her in many ways that he cared, but he'd also hurt her feelings.

Jonathan folded his arms more tightly around her. "You're shivering."

"That's because it's freezing."

"I think it's because you want me as much as I want you."

"Sex won't solve anything."

"It won't hurt anything, either. Sherry, let me love you."

"What? You mean—here."

"It's the hot spot of the Hardison Ranch. More romantic trysts have taken place in this old barn than you can imagine. Not mine, of course," he added hastily. "My brothers. You know how Jeff and Wade are."

She knew them now as devoted partners to their women, but she knew that domestic tranquility hadn't come cheap. They'd both had to work pretty hard at it.

Jonathan was working hard, too. But she still had serious doubts about whether she was the right woman for him—even when he was kissing her neck, like he was now, and running his hands along her back and under the edge of her sweater.

Every cell in her body screamed for the closeness he could bring, the intimacy—real intimacy—she'd had so little of in her life.

Against her better judgment, Sherry melted. She forgot the way he'd fired her when she didn't fit in just perfectly. She forgot his fits of temper and crankiness, and the way he'd judged her over her decision to give up Charlie as a baby. She swept all those things from her mind and focused only on what she saw in his eyes, glinting dark in the dim light from the flashlight.

God help her, he did love her. She saw that, believed that, and she knew this time she wasn't deluding herself, seeing what she wanted to see. This was real. And she responded to it far more easily than she would have to the most practiced seduction.

"Oh, Jonathan," she said on a sigh. "What am I going to do with you?" She wound her arms around his neck and kissed him with all the passion in her heart, in her soul.

Chapter Thirteen

Funny, but Sherry didn't feel cold anymore. An inner fire had flared to life, warming her from her core outward.

Before she could get too carried away with the kissing, she stopped and asked, "What about Charlie? And Anne? Where did they go?"

"Before I came into the barn, I told Anne to take Charlie back to camp and leave me alone with you, that we had things to talk about."

"Oh, good." Suddenly she didn't care if Jonathan's entire family knew they were making love in the old barn. He was right—this was good. It felt soothing, healing even, to have Jonathan kissing her with so much passion, yet with such reverence, as if she were a wild creature he was afraid would flee if he made any sudden moves.

But then he did make a sudden move—he swung her up into his arms.

She shrieked in protest. "Jonathan! You can't do that. Your leg, you'll hurt—"

"Watch me." At least he didn't carry her far, only to the nearest stack of hay bales. He moved with surprising agility for a man with a leg in a cast. He set her down, took off his down-filled jacket and laid it over the hay. "Hay can be scratchy."

"How would you know? Since you never carried on out here like your wayward brothers."

He chuckled. "I've just heard, that's all." He guided her to sit on his jacket. "I'd kneel down to take off your shoes, but that's very nearly impossible."

"Then just…" She held out her arms to him.

They kissed and stroked and murmured to each other on the bed of hay, which was surprisingly comfortable, until their hands had warmed against each other's flesh and their steaming breath had warmed the air around them. Since she'd been so reluctant at first, Sherry took the initiative, unbuttoning Jonathan's flannel shirt. She didn't try to remove it, fearful that he'd freeze, but contented herself with caressing his firm chest and rubbing the hair-roughened surface with her cheek.

He was so…masculine.

A surge of desire shot through her, making her impatient. Jonathan was far more mobile than when they'd first made love and more aggressive, though still gentle. He pushed her down and put his hands inside her sweater. In moments he had the front clasp of her bra unfastened and had filled his hands with both breasts.

He groaned and kissed her some more, insinuating the knee of his good leg between her thighs and exerting an exquisite pressure there.

All Sherry could think about was getting her jeans

off and pulling him closer. She wanted those strong, masculine hands on her bare skin. She wanted to hold his hardness in her hands and give him pleasure. Her heart was full to bursting with a sudden rush of emotion for this man who'd laid it all on the line for her, opened himself up, made himself vulnerable.

She wanted to somehow make up for the fact that she hadn't responded to his love the way any sane woman ought to, falling at his feet in a swoon.

Sherry fumbled with the fastening on Jonathan's jeans. He pulled away from her just long enough to yank off his one shoe, then take off his jeans and briefs, gasping as the cool night air struck all the places that didn't like to be cold.

But the night air couldn't quench his passion. A blizzard couldn't have. In the time it took to maneuver his jeans over the cast, Sherry had wiggled out of hers and kicked them aside, though she still wore a pair of silky black panties.

"Mmm, is that what you wear for everyday?"

"No, this morning I thought, 'Hey, I bet some man will see me in my underwear today. I'll wear the black.' Of *course* it's what I wear every day. I don't own any boring panties. No makeover was going to change that."

"Good. Let's see how they look flying through the air." He proceeded to demonstrate, sliding the panties down Sherry's long, silky legs. They were splendid, firm and creamy. He spent a few precious moments just admiring them—until he realized she had goose bumps. The poor girl was freezing.

He stretched out beside her, shielding her from the

cold as best he could without crushing her with his cast. That meant straddling her, pressing his already turgid erection against the soft triangle of curls at the apex of her thighs.

He groaned. He'd been groaning a lot. Something about making love in the cold, and Sherry feeling so warm and inviting, the slight discomfort paired with the excruciating pleasure of being close to such an incredible woman, was the biggest turn-on of his life.

Or maybe it was the fact that he'd fallen in love with her. He'd surprised himself when he'd admitted that out loud, but he'd instantly realized it was true. Not even the mother of his children had captured his heart so thoroughly.

Sherry shifted one of her legs so she could open for him. ''I can't wait any longer,'' she said bluntly, reaching down to guide him home. He held himself poised at her entrance, savoring that first delicious contact. She raised her hips to envelop him, and he found himself thrusting deeply inside her as they both sighed with satisfaction.

He moved slowly at first, wanting this brief interlude to last as long as possible. He knew damn well it might be their last time together. He varied his tempo, bringing himself and Sherry almost to a peak, then slowing, then revving up again until she was crying his name.

He would never forget the sound of her passion-filled voice, his name on her lips, claiming him. He released his tenuous control, and she bit him on the shoulder as she climaxed. Moments later she kissed the little pink teeth marks she'd left on his skin. He couldn't be sure, as the flashlight batteries were failing and the light growing dimmer, but he thought he saw tears in her eyes.

He knew then that she was saying goodbye to him.

SHERRY WASN'T SURE how they would get back to the house. Jonathan's recovery had escalated dramatically, but there was no way he could walk back. It was at least a quarter mile.

"I'll go get a car and come back for you," she offered.

"I can make it," he said stubbornly. But when they exited the barn, their problem was solved. Anne and Charlie had left the ATV for them.

"Well, that was thoughtful," Sherry said as she climbed into the driver's seat. "I'll have to bake them a cake." It was easier to make small talk than to acknowledge what had just happened.

She'd silently sworn that making love to Jonathan wouldn't solve anything, wouldn't change anything. But it had changed something inside her. She couldn't seem to rile herself up anymore. Her righteous indignation had crumbled. She could hardly remember what he'd done to upset her so much. She could only remember his gentle touch, the way he'd tried to protect her from the cold and the way he'd held her afterward for a long, long time, savoring the afterglow.

"You must be hungry," he said. "You didn't get to eat your turkey sandwich."

"To tell you the truth, after cooking four turkeys and eating a plateful this afternoon, turkey just doesn't do it for me."

"How about an omelette?"

"Are you offering to cook for me?"

"Sure."

"No," she said flatly. "I don't want to see you standing on that leg again tonight, and maybe not tomorrow. If I'm hungry, I'll find something."

"Yes, Nurse Nancy."

"I hate it when people call me that," she warned.

"You know I'm teasing. You're a wonderful nurse. I told Jeff and my dad you'd be a fine addition to their practice."

"Jonathan, don't—"

"I'm not trying to pressure you," he said. "I promised I wouldn't and I won't."

They were silent for a while as Sherry negotiated a particularly challenging series of gopher holes and considered her next words.

"I'm going to ask Anne to help me apply to adopt Charlie," she said, essentially admitting Jonathan had been right all along.

"I know. I heard the last part of your conversation with him. It's a pretty big decision. If I can help with anything, offer advice, or even financial assistance, please ask." He didn't gloat or point out his victory.

"It changes everything," she said. "My life will never be the same."

"That's how I felt when Sam was born. You'll find you're stronger than you imagined you could be."

"I'm not worried about me so much as Charlie. It will be a huge adjustment for him. During the transition, I want to keep things as stable as possible for him."

His suspicions had been correct. She was leaving him. "I get it, Sherry. Charlie will have enough on his plate dealing with a new mother and a new home. Throwing Mom's boyfriend and his kids into the mix, not to mention a long-distance romance, would be too stressful—especially if you and I are trying to figure out how to fit our lives together."

"Then you understand?"

"I understand, but I don't agree. I think it's foolish to throw away what we've got. Besides, I think it might be good for Charlie to spend more time in the country—maybe even to live here full-time. It's done wonders for him so far."

"Maybe…in a while. When things settle down and I get my life back in order."

"Does anybody ever get their life back in order? While you're waiting around for that to happen, life passes you by."

She made no reply to that.

"I guess I'm trying to make your decisions for you again, huh?"

"The thought had crossed my mind." But there was no resentment in her voice.

"Just hit me on the head with a stick. I'll learn eventually." He paused, hating that they were almost back to the house. He didn't know when or if he would be with her again. "When are you leaving?"

"I'll go back to the camp tonight. Back to Dallas Sunday, when Charlie leaves."

So soon. It was much too soon. Jonathan felt her slipping away from him like sand through his fingers, and there wasn't a damn thing he could do about it.

How ironic that the one thing he'd wanted her to do—
take responsibility for her son—was the one thing that
guaranteed she and Jonathan couldn't be together.

BACK AT THE HOUSE Jonathan said nothing about
Sherry's decision to adopt Charlie, though he was
buoyed by the news that she wanted to keep her son.
He would let her tell whomever she chose, whenever
she chose.

Still, he watched her closely those first few minutes
to see what she would do. Of course, the first thing
she did was apologize to everyone for worrying them.
She found Pete, Sally, Jeff, Allison, Edward, Anne
and Charlie in the den, watching TV, seemingly un-
concerned about Sherry's return. Jonathan suspected
they had all decided not to make a big to-do over
Sherry, so as not to further embarrass her.

He had a pretty amazing family. He sure wished
he knew how to make Sherry a permanent part of it.

"...and once the ladder fell, I was stuck," she explained.

But she wasn't going to trust him with her heart,
not now for sure—maybe not ever.

SHERRY MADE IT through the rest of the camp with
few incidents. Now that she had the cooking routine
down, she could do it in her sleep, and she spent more
time with the kids. After her confession at the barn
on Thanksgiving, they'd come to view her as more
than just the cook. The girls, especially, were asking
her a lot of questions and listening carefully to her
responses.

On Sunday Wade staged a minirodeo so the kids could showcase their newly acquired talents, complete with blue ribbons for the winners—and Wade made sure every kid won at something. Sherry sniffled with maternal pride when Charlie actually managed to get a rope around a calf's neck and wrestle it to the ground, earning him a first place in that event.

Then the minibuses arrived to take the kids home. Sherry wanted to yank each one of them back as they climbed onto the vehicles, some of the younger ones crying openly. She knew what awaited some of them when they got home, and it wasn't pretty.

Charlie didn't climb on a bus. Carla came to get him and take him to his new foster home, which he didn't seem too thrilled about.

"Am I gonna see you ever again?" he asked Sherry, completely serious.

"Of course! Anne is already working on the forms I'll need to apply for the adoption, and our first visitation is set up for next Saturday." Her heart ached for him. A lot of people must have broken a lot of promises for him to be so skeptical.

"Okay." He shook hands with Wade. "Thanks, Wade. I had a good time."

Again Sherry felt pride. His manners had improved this past week. Or maybe he had them all along and just chose not to display them before.

"It was my pleasure. Anytime Sherry wants to bring you out to practice riding and roping, just let me know."

Sherry shot him a grateful smile. This was not an

offer he extended to all of the campers. She couldn't believe how generous the Hardisons had been with her and with Charlie.

When the two buses left and the last of the dust settled on the driveway, Sherry knew it was time for her to leave, too. Though she half wished Jonathan would come over to say goodbye and wish her well, she was sort of grateful he didn't. She needed time away from him, time to get settled into her new life in Dallas, take a deep breath and figure out what she really wanted, what was really best for her and Charlie.

You want Jonathan, her obstinate inner voice said.

The voice spoke the truth. But maybe, with time and distance, her craving for him would diminish and she could think straight again.

That thought hardly gave her solace.

She stuffed everything back into her Firebird—she couldn't believe the amount of clothes and cosmetics she'd brought with her for a week on a ranch. It seemed silly now, even if all her primping *had* gotten Jonathan's attention.

When she was finished packing, Wade and Anne walked outside with her to say goodbye.

"You really were a lifesaver," Anne said. "I hadn't realized that Sally might want some time off when she got home from her honeymoon. Your filling in solved so many problems."

"Oh, come on, you all came to my rescue and you know it. Taking Charlie in at the last minute, giving me a place to stay and a way to visit with him—I can't think of any words to thank you."

"You can thank us by coming back to visit."

"I intend to."

"Really? Do you really?" Anne asked earnestly. Sherry knew what she actually meant. Was she going to work things out with Jonathan?

"I *will* try," she assured Anne. She thought that would be the end of it. She hugged Anne, gave Wade a kiss on the cheek and started to climb into her car.

Suddenly Wade, who'd been silent during the exchange, spoke up. "Can I tell Jonathan anything for you?"

Sherry thought for a few moments. "Yeah. Tell him to take care of Trouble."

Wade grinned, but the smile quickly faded. "You know, when Anne and I couldn't work things out, I left, too. I thought distance was the only answer. But it's impossible to work through any problems if you don't talk. I wouldn't have figured that out if Anne hadn't come after my stubborn hide."

Sherry smiled sadly. She couldn't picture Jonathan coming after her the way Anne had gone after Wade, flying in the middle of the night to Kansas City when Wade was injured in a rodeo there.

"I'm not running away," she said firmly. "I'm taking a deep breath, that's all."

Still, as she drove away from the camp, past the ranch, and onto the highway that would take her away from Cottonwood, she couldn't help glancing in the rearview mirror over and over.

THREE DAYS AFTER Sherry's departure, Jonathan was still in a state of shock. He'd known she was leaving, but some part of him hadn't honestly believed she would go. How could she leave him when she loved him and she knew he loved her?

He'd *told* her he loved her. Did she not believe him? Did she not understand that a man like him didn't love easily? He'd opened his heart to her, something he hadn't done since his love for Rita had been so abused.

And she'd stomped it flat.

"Daddy, when is Sherry coming back?" Kristin asked innocently at the dinner table Wednesday evening.

"Yeah, ain't that a good question," Pete said.

Sally flicked him with a dishcloth as she set a hot casserole on the table. "Old man, don't rile him. It's not like *you* set a shining example for him."

"I'm never gonna hear the end of this, am I?" Pete groused. "You're the one who wouldn't commit."

"Only because I wasn't psychic. How was I supposed to know 'I like your mashed potatoes' was a marriage proposal?" But she softened the comment with an indulgent smile.

"Really, Daddy," Kristin persisted. "When is she coming back?"

Sam tugged at one of his sister's pigtails. "She's not coming back, dope. She's like Mom. She doesn't want to live on a ranch."

Instinctively Jonathan knew his son's assessment of Sherry was wrong. Though she'd needed a few days to adjust, Sherry had taken to small-town living like a flea takes to a dog. She'd found a true sense of family here. She'd made friends.

But life was about choices, and Sherry had made hers. "Sherry has a life back in Dallas," Jonathan explained. "She cares about us, but now that she's adopting Charlie, she has her own family to worry about."

Undeterred, Kristin tugged her dad's sleeve. "Can we go visit her, then? Like we go and visit Mom in New Orleans?"

"Um, I don't know about that, doodlebug. Your mom is, well, your mom, and that means you *should* spend time with her."

"But Sherry's more fun than mom," Kristin said matter-of-factly. "I'd rather visit her."

"But she hasn't invited us," Jonathan pointed out sensibly.

"So? I could call her and ask her to invite us."

"No, don't do that," Jonathan said hastily. He'd promised he wouldn't pressure Sherry to make any decisions where he was concerned. Besides, he couldn't just up and visit Sherry. A trip to Dallas would disrupt his whole life. He would have to arrange for someone to take over his duties on the ranch, which he'd shunned enough in recent weeks.

"Why not?" Kristin wanted to know.

"Because they had a big fight," Sam said with an impatient sigh. "After grown-ups have a big fight, they don't want to see each other anymore."

"It's not that I don't want to see her," Jonathan

corrected Sam. "I...care for Sherry a great deal. It's just that..."

"Why don't you just get married?" Kristin asked, obviously frustrated by her inability to understand the obtuse world of adults.

"Yeah, why don't you?" Pete echoed, earning a censorious stare from Sally.

Suddenly Jonathan saw things clearly. He got it. It wasn't just that he judged Sherry or criticized her. He had expected her to do all the changing, make all the effort. He'd been unwilling to rearrange *his* life to accommodate her, as if his life was more important than hers. She'd tried to tell him that, but he'd been too pigheaded to see it.

"Jonathan, is something wrong?" Sally asked.

"No, no, I'm great. Or I will be, if I can make things right."

Oh, God, he'd been such an idiot. He'd told Sherry he loved her, but had he done anything to prove it? Other than expecting her to rearrange her life to be with him? Give up a high-paying job, friends, her parents, yank Charlie out of whatever school he was in, give up the prospect of having more children, all for the pleasure of his company?

Hell, when he'd asked Rita to do most of that stuff, at least he'd offered her a wedding ring. For the first time, he realized the failure of his marriage to Rita just might not have been all her fault.

Pete chuckled. "You look like someone just hit you over the head with a sledgehammer."

"That's what I feel like," he said with a growing

sense of wonder. How had it taken him so long to see the truth? Why had no one ever told him he was being such a turkey?

Aw, hell. Would he have listened if someone had tried?

"All right," he said with decisiveness. "We'll go visit Sherry."

"When?" Kristin demanded, not intending to let her father weasel out of this one.

"This weekend. We'll surprise her."

"You're not even going to call and give her warning?" Sally asked.

"No. I'm not going to give her a chance to say no until she's heard everything I have to say, face-to-face." He also wasn't above using his children. Sherry had a soft spot for them, and who could resist Kristin's pleading eyes?

SHERRY WOKE UP early the following Saturday morning despite the fact she'd lain awake far into the night. But who could sleep on her infernal sofa bed? She tossed and turned until the sun started to shine through her living room window, then gave up and threw the covers off.

A cup of coffee would put her right.

She started the coffeepot, then peeked in on her overnight guest. Charlie was snoozing peacefully, looking a little ridiculous amidst the ruffles and bows and flounces of Sherry's feminine bed linens. But she'd wanted his first weekend with her to be fun and memorable—memorable not for the permanent kink he would get in his back if she forced him to sleep on the sofa bed. So she'd gallantly put him in her own room.

She had an appointment with a real estate agent later today to look at some properties. Anne stressed it was imperative for her to have a private bedroom for Charlie in order to be considered a fit adoptive mother.

She'd just taken her first sip of coffee, savoring the flavor, when her doorbell rang. Who would be bothering her this early? she wondered, irritated. She was sure she still had creases in her face from her pillow.

She peeked through her peephole and was shocked to see Jonathan Hardison's face. And he was smiling.

"Just a minute!" she called as she chanced a look at herself in the entry hall mirror. *Oh, my God.* Well, she couldn't just leave him on her front porch while she primped. He would have to take her as she was. But wasn't that the main lesson she'd learned during her time in Cottonwood? That all those outward trimmings didn't matter?

Still, thirty-one years' worth of vanity was hard to erase.

She flung the door open and was immediately assaulted by an airborne seven-year-old, who leaped into her arms.

"Surprise!" all three of them greeted her—Kristin, Sam and Jonathan.

Sherry hugged Kristin back. She felt so good, this sweet child who had grown to love Sherry when

Sherry had done little to earn it. Kristin was just that way.

Remembering Charlie asleep in her bedroom, Sherry held a finger to her lips to quiet the kids' excited chatter about leaving at five this morning. "Shh! Some people are still sleeping."

Kristin clamped a hand over her mouth. "Who else is here?" she asked, the words slipping out between her fingers.

Sam grinned. "I'll bet it's Charlie!"

Chapter Fourteen

"Oh. Charlie." Jonathan smiled, though sheepishly. "I'm sorry we barged in on you when you're visiting with your son. We can come back—"

"No, don't you dare. Charlie will be happy to see you, especially the kids. I think he's already tired of me," she admitted.

"Don't take it personally," Jonathan said. "I hear most twelve-year-olds could make a career out of hating their parents. If he's bristling over all the attention you're giving him, then he's acting just like Wade did at that age."

"Can we go wake him up?" Sam asked.

Sherry hesitated. Her visit with Charlie had gone pretty smoothly so far, but she was still a bundle of nerves now that she had responsibility for him.

She was saved from answering when the bedroom door opened and Charlie appeared in a T-shirt and boxers, yawning. "What the hell's going on in here?"

"Charlie!" Sherry scolded. She'd been working on toning down his language, but he still forgot sometimes.

"Oops, sorry." Then he smiled. "Hey, Sam. Hi, doodlebug."

Kristin sighed in exasperation. "Don't *you* start calling me that, too. I'm not a bug!" But it was clear she liked the endearment.

"Charlie, why don't you put on some clothes and then show Sam and Kristin your new game? Then you can let them play while you get showered. Breakfast should be ready by then."

"Okay."

All three kids disappeared into the bedroom, leaving Sherry and Jonathan alone.

"Well," she said as she poured Jonathan a cup of coffee. "This is a surprise."

"I would have called first, but I didn't want to give you the chance to tell me not to come."

"I couldn't have done that. I've missed you too much." She realized Jonathan was still standing in the doorway to her tiny kitchen. "For heaven's sake, sit down. It's amazing your leg hasn't simply fallen off, the way you abuse it." She pulled out a stool for him at the breakfast bar, which had a view into the kitchen. She could work while they talked. It was much safer if she kept her hands occupied, not to mention having a countertop and sink between them.

She went to work on cinnamon rolls, dumping the ingredients into a bowl and mixing it with a wooden spoon. She waited to see if Jonathan would volunteer the reason for his visit.

"I know I said I'd give you time," he finally began. "But I'm impatient, how much time do you need? How long will it take for your life to settle down?''

She looked up from her work and smiled mischievously. "Not that long, I guess." Then she focused again on her cooking, dumping the dough onto the flour-covered countertop and kneading it. She knew her face was turning pink because she could feel the heat.

She was such a pushover. For the life of her, she couldn't remember why she'd felt it was so important to leave Cottonwood.

"You'll be happy to know your orphan calf is eating on his own, now. He'll be returning to the herd soon."

"Good. Now aren't you glad you invested all that effort to fix him up?"

"Yeah, okay, you were right. Never thought I'd say this about a cow, but he is kind of cute." Jonathan cleared his throat. "So, is now a good time to talk about the future?"

Sherry gulped, then nodded. Her heart pounded in her ears.

"What's the real estate market like up here? Could I buy a four-bedroom house for a couple hundred thousand?"

"Depends on the neighborhood—huh?" Why was he talking about real estate?

"Well, we need four bedrooms. One for each of the kids, and one for us. If we have more babies, the kids will have to double up, but Kristin would love a little—"

"Whoa, whoa!" She gave up on the dough. Was

she hearing things? "You want to move to Dallas. And live in a house. With me and an indeterminate number of children."

"I thought we might get married first."

Sherry's head spun. She felt the way she had when she'd first opened the door on Charlie and realized he was her son, though at least she didn't pass out this time.

"You're not just teasing me, right?" She felt as dull-witted as a bear that just woke up from hibernation.

"Sherry, darlin', I wouldn't tease about a thing like marriage. A couple of days ago I finally realized how lousy I was treating you. I understood why you left. I *got it.*"

"I'm not sure *I* even get it." She came around the wall so she could be within touching distance of him. To hell with being safe. "I second-guessed myself a million times after I left. If we love each other, isn't love supposed to conquer all?"

"I'm not sure it can conquer your boyfriend being a selfish bastard. I was expecting you to do all the changing. I wanted you to disrupt *your* life, sell your condo, move to be near me, take a less interesting, lower paying job—and give up the prospect of having babies. I wanted you to play surrogate mother to my children, but I never offered to be a father to yours.

"You were so right about me. I was inflexible, judgmental, self-righteous—"

"Hey, hey, easy there on the self-flagellation." She put her arms around him. She couldn't help herself. "None of us is perfect. I think we've proved that."

"I'm turning over a new leaf." He started to melt into the embrace, but then, as if he were overtaken by a new determination, he grasped her shoulders so he could look her in the eye. "I'm going to be tolerant and flexible, I swear it. But I know words aren't enough to convince you. I have to prove myself. So my first action as a flexible, nonjudgmental sort of guy is to move to Dallas."

"But—"

"The second thing I'll do is look into a vasectomy reversal. Doctors can do amazing things with lasers these days. If that doesn't work, I'm okay with the idea of a sperm bank."

Sherry was having a hard time finding words, she was so overwhelmed. Jonathan had just offered her one of the most precious things he could have—his willingness to be a father to Charlie. The only thing she could think to ask was, "What about your ranch?"

"I can hire someone to run the ranch. Cal Chandler is a smart guy. He could do it, with a little guidance from Granddad."

"But—"

"It'll still mean you'll have to move...."

"I was going to do that, anyway. I need room for Charlie."

"But you can keep your job."

"I don't care about the job. It's dreadful. I was ready to turn in my resignation after the first day. The doctor is an egomaniac, and the other nurses there— I call them the wardrobe police. They didn't like my Scooby-doo scrubs." She was babbling, she knew, because she was completely overwhelmed. She could almost imagine she was dreaming this, except Jonathan's hands on her arms felt too warm, too strong, too real to be a dream. She could smell him, that wonderful combination of soap and bleach and leather that was his alone.

Her dreams were never this vivid.

Her blathering had momentarily derailed him. "Well, you can find another job," he offered, as if this were the only issue.

"Are Jeff and Edward still looking for a nurse?"

"Yes, but, Sherry, that's the whole point. You don't have to move to Cottonwood and make all these changes for me. I'm willing to change for you."

"Yes, Jonathan, I get it. But I don't want you to change. You'd go insane living in a big city. And what would Kristin do without her pony?"

"I wouldn't go insane as long as you were with me."

He meant it. Lord help her, he was as sincere as her coffee was strong. This wasn't some maneuver to get her to conform to his expectations. He really was willing to move away from his family and give up his wonderful home, his work, his heritage, just to be with her and with her son.

Well, hell, could he have given her better proof that he loved her?

"Jonathan, I fell in love with a rancher. And I want to marry a rancher. I want to move to Cottonwood and raise my son on a ranch...."

"I sense a 'but.'"

"But don't you think three children are enough?"

she blurted out, a little desperately. "I love kids, but I'm floundering here with this motherhood thing. You actually want a *baby?*"

"I thought *you* did. Or that you might."

"Well, let's not rush into anything. Three is about all I can handle for now." Although, if she stopped to think about it, the idea of having a baby with Jonathan made her heart skip a beat.

"Does that mean you'll think about it? Marrying me?"

"Oh, Jonathan, don't you realize I've been thinking about marrying you since I first saw you? I don't have to think about it anymore. Of course I'll marry you. But..."

"You're worried about how Charlie will take it."

"Yes, exactly. I know you're not supposed to let your kids dictate how you live your life. I've been reading every parenting book I can get my hands on. But there've been so many changes for him already. I don't want him to think I'm pushing him aside to make room for a husband and two more kids."

"I understand."

"You do?"

"I've been giving this a lot of thought. I've thought through all the repercussions. And how our marriage would affect Charlie is one of my concerns, too. Will you let me talk to him?"

She nodded as a feeling of awe crept over her. She was starting to believe this all just might work out. "Send Sam and Kristin in here. They can help me with the cinnamon buns."

JONATHAN COULDN'T HELP smiling when he entered Sherry's bedroom. He should have expected as much. He'd never seen so much pink, and the bed was about to choke on its own ruffles. When they shared a bedroom, he hoped she wouldn't do it up like this. But if she wanted to, he swore he wouldn't say a word.

"Look, Dad, I'm up to ten thousand points," Sam said as he used a computer mouse to defend earth against invading spacecraft. Immediately after his announcement, his rocket got blown up.

"See, you shouldn't brag," Kristin gloated.

"Okay, guys, Sherry wants help in the kitchen. I need to talk to Charlie privately."

The kids went without a single grumble. Maybe they sensed how important the next few minutes were to their future.

Charlie, who'd pulled on a pair of jeans, looked at him dubiously. The kid was actually not bad looking, now that he'd dropped a few pounds and wore clothes that fit. He had a new haircut, too.

"New glasses?" Jonathan asked to break the ice.

"Yeah. Sherry bought 'em. She's kind of in to buying things for me." Charlie indicated a pile of toys and clothes stacked in a corner of the room.

"Guess she's trying to make up for lost time," Jonathan said.

"Yeah. It's kind of funny. I told her she didn't have to, but she just keeps whipping out that credit card."

"She's showing you she loves you."

"Yeah, I know."

Conversation ground to a halt. Jonathan wasn't sure

how to say what he needed to. Then Charlie started it for him.

"You want me out of the way, I guess."

"What? Oh, no, Charlie, that's not it at all."

"It's okay, I get it. If not for me showing up, you and Sherry would be all cozy by now. I messed up your plans."

"No. That's not true. If anything, you brought us together."

Charlie wasn't buying it. "She walked out on you 'cause of me. I got eyes."

"Listen to me. You don't know the whole story. Part of having a good relationship means learning to weather the ups and downs and to deal with the unexpected. You showing up forced us to learn some things about each other, and about ourselves."

Charlie looked at him warily.

"I want to marry your mom. But I also want to adopt you."

The boy still said nothing.

"I'd like you both to come live with me on the ranch. I want you to be a big brother to Sam and Kristin. But if you think that's too many changes all at one time, we can take things slowly. We can live here."

"All of us? Here?" He looked around the small bedroom.

"No, in a house. A big house. But here in Dallas."

"Why would we do that when you already have a house?"

This wasn't going quite as well as Jonathan had hoped. "So when Sherry and I get married, it won't disrupt things so much. She wants you to be happy. We both do. You're the most important person in her life.''

''She said that?''

''She didn't have to. It's pretty clear. You guys are a package deal. But that's okay, because I want you both. So it's up to you, buddy. What do you think? Can we all be a family?''

Charlie turned away. ''You don't even know me.''

''I know you a little bit. You remind me of my brother Wade. He was a rebel, kind of like you.''

He turned back. ''You think I'm like Wade?'' He was definitely intrigued with that idea.

''And I know you're good with Sam and Kristin. You're very patient with them, and they like you. And you're smart. You learn things quick. You're basically a good kid. What else do I need to know?''

''I'm not really a good kid,'' he said glumly.

''Of course you are. Maybe you've taken a few wrong turns here and there, but deep down you're good. I know that much. We can work on the rest. So, how about it?''

Charlie flashed a mischievous smile. ''Will I get my own horse?''

''Absolutely.''

''I was gonna say yes, anyway.''

''Good man.'' Jonathan offered Charlie his hand. Charlie took it, then unexpectedly gave him a quick hug.

WHILE THE cinnamon rolls baked, Sherry fixed bacon and eggs. She didn't want anyone to go hungry. Jonathan watched her, amazed at how comfortable she was with his kids and how quickly she'd learned how to be a mother to Charlie. No one would guess they'd known each other only a couple of weeks.

She'd learned a lot about Jonathan, too. The eggs were firm, he noticed—just the way he liked them. Or was he starting to like eggs any old way Sherry made them?

He'd said nothing to her after his talk with Charlie. He wanted time alone with her, so he could do this thing up right.

They all gorged on the sumptuous breakfast, topping it off with warm cinnamon rolls.

"Okay, now," Sherry said as she started to clear the table. "Nothing like a little exercise to burn off all these calories we just ate. Charlie, I want you to take Sam and Kristin down to the lake to feed the ducks, and then to the playground. Okay?"

Charlie gave her a knowing look. "No problem. How long do you need us to be gone?"

The question flustered Sherry, so Jonathan answered for her. "An hour should do it."

Charlie winked. "Don't blow it, man."

As soon as the kids cleared out, Jonathan wasted no time. He found Kristin's pink plastic purse, which featured Princess Pony, and tucked it under his arm. He looked at Sherry. "Come with me."

Her eyes brimming with anticipation, Sherry followed him into her bedroom. He guided her to the dresser and turned her to face it.

"What are you doing?" she asked.

He opened the purse and pulled out his mother's

antique comb, the one that had caused such an uproar the morning after he and Sherry first made love.

"I think I might've told you before," Jonathan said as he finger-combed her mass of tangled curls, "that this comb belonged to my mother. She gave it to me shortly before she died and said I was to present it to that one special woman in my life."

"And you gave it to Rita."

"Big mistake. Have you ever seen Rita or a picture of her?"

"No."

"Her hair is about one inch long all over. Very sophisticated. Very chic."

Sherry grinned. "But she can't wear a comb."

Jonathan piled Sherry's blond curls on top of her head and worked the comb in. "Frankly, you're the only woman I know with enough hair to make this work. So the comb must be meant for you. And I guess that means we'll have to get married. Will you marry me, Sherry?"

"What did Charlie say?"

"He's fine with the whole thing. Well, okay...I bribed him with a horse."

"You don't believe in bribing children."

"I'm beginning to see the merits." He turned serious. "Come on, Sherry, what do you say?"

She slid her hands around his neck and pulled him down for a long, wet kiss.

"That would be...yes?"

"Yes."

Epilogue

It looked as if the whole town of Cottonwood had turned out for the double Hardison Christmas Eve wedding. Jonathan hadn't seen the church this packed since Wade and Anne's wedding, and then half the guests were friends of the Chatsworths from Dallas.

Sherry had brought her own small contingent from the city—her parents, her nursing school friends and a couple of neighbors. She'd even invited Charlie's new foster parents and his social worker, with whom she'd apparently grown close in a short time. No surprise there.

But the rest of the wedding guests were home-grown Cottonwoodites. He was pretty sure at least half of them hadn't been invited—they'd just come to witness one of the most improbable events in Cottonwood history. Not one, but two of the unmarriageable Hardison brothers were tying the knot simultaneously.

When news of Jonathan and Sherry's engagement had broken, Allison and Jeff had immediately offered to include them in their wedding. Sherry had declined at first, not wanting to steal the other couple's thunder. But Allison had persuaded her that it would be more fun to share the festivities with two couples. Plus she had a seamstress who could whip up any sort of wedding gown Sherry could dream up in less than a week.

Jonathan had been all for the Christmas wedding. Hell, he would have preferred to elope with Sherry—the sooner the better. So Sherry had finally given in.

Now that the time was approaching, Jonathan felt a little nervous. Though he'd grown more accustomed to parties, due to Sherry's diligent efforts, he wasn't thrilled about the idea of speaking his vows in front of a throng of people, many of them strangers. Shouldn't a wedding be more private?

At five minutes to three, the militant wedding planner ushered him and Jeff, along with the groomsmen, to the front of the church by way of a side aisle.

"Good luck, fellas," said Edward. "Better you than me."

"You're next," Jonathan warned him.

Edward just laughed. "Weddings might be contagious, but I've been vaccinated."

Jonathan walked with hardly a limp to the front of the church. His father had fitted him with a special, lightweight walking cast that fit inside the leg of his tuxedo pants, just for the occasion. Another couple of weeks and the cast would come off altogether.

"You nervous?" Jeff asked him.

"I'm only about to throw up."

"Me, too. How did we get talked into this dog and pony show?"

"When you're in love, you can get talked into almost anything."

"Guess that's it."

"Hi, Daddy! Hi, Uncle Jeff!"

Jonathan saw Kristin waving to them from the front pew. She sat between Sam and Charlie. The sight of the three of them, a perfect symbol of their new, blended family, brought a lump to his throat.

He waved back to Kristin and nodded when Charlie gave him a thumbs-up. Jonathan couldn't wait until tomorrow morning. Wade was riding over to the ranch on Charlie's Christmas present, a gentle gelding the boy had seemed fond of during rodeo camp. Kristin, who'd outgrown her Shetland pony, was getting a new horse, as well. Sam had gotten a new horse for his birthday last summer, so he was getting the puppy he'd been asking for since he could talk.

As for his lovely soon-to-be wife, she was getting a shiny red pickup truck, though he didn't imagine she would part company with her precious, impractical Firebird anytime soon.

When the organ music suddenly got louder, Jonathan found it hard to breathe.

"Steady, bro," Jeff said with a nervous laugh.

"You should talk. Your fingers are going to fall off if you clench your fists any tighter."

The bridesmaids, who included Anne, walked down the aisle in stately forest-green velvet, their hair adorned with holly.

"Jeez, could they walk any slower?" Jonathan whispered.

Jeff nudged him. Reverend Crane, soon to be Jeff's father-in-law, glared at him.

Finally the brides appeared. First Allison, escorted by her uncle, glided down the aisle in a simple dress of white velvet. She wore a crown of holly, like some pagan goddess.

"Wow," was all Jeff said.

Next came Sherry—in a dress with a hoop skirt. It was covered with lace and seed pearls and scallops. Her veil, made of yards and yards of netting, trailed to the ground. Her hair, all those glorious golden curls, cascaded from the top of the veil like a waterfall.

Sherry never did anything halfway. On any other woman, the dress would have been ridiculous. But on Sherry it looked grand.

Jonathan didn't remember much of what followed, except for the part where he got to kiss Sherry. He tried to keep it chaste, but it was difficult, since all he could think about was peeling off all those layers of satin and netting. He'd always thought she was beautiful, but today she was radiant, a princess bride, a sassy Cinderella marrying her prince.

And he was the prince, at least for a day. But only because Sherry had kissed the frog. They'd both been transformed—and his transformation had been the most dramatic, the most wonderful. After all, Sherry had been pretty wonderful the whole time.

At the reception, it seemed everyone wanted to dance with the brides, so Jeff and Jonathan found themselves hanging out by the punch bowl. Before long, Wade joined them, and then Pete.

"Well, here we are," Wade said. "Those hardened, Hardison bachelors. Who would have thought, when I came back to town last year, we'd all be married by this Christmas?"

"It just took the right women," Jonathan said. Then he nodded toward the dance floor, where Edward was doing the polka with none other than Sherry's mother. They were both laughing as they misstepped, nearly tripping over each other's feet.

"Haven't seen Ed laugh like that in a long time," Pete commented as he poured himself a glass of punch.

The three brothers looked at each other. Then they all grinned. Their father, a widower for umpteen years, might *think* he was immune to weddings. But he simply needed to meet another woman who knew how to marry a Hardison.

HARLEQUIN®

AMERICAN *Romance®*

Bestselling author
Muriel Jensen
kicks off

MILLIONAIRE, MONTANA

beginning in January 2003 with
JACKPOT BABY

Welcome to Millionaire, Montana, where twelve lucky
townspeople have won a multimillion-dollar jackpot.
And where one millionaire in particular has just...
found a baby on her doorstep.

The excitement continues with:

BIG-BUCKS BACHELOR by Leah Vale
on-sale February 2003

SURPRISE INHERITANCE by Charlotte Douglas
on-sale March 2003

FOUR-KARAT FIANCÉE by Sharon Swan
on-sale April 2003

PRICELESS MARRIAGE by Bonnie Gardner
on-sale May 2003

FORTUNE'S TWINS by Kara Lennox
on-sale June 2003

Available at your favorite retail outlet.

HARLEQUIN®
Makes any time special®

HARJB

Steeple Hill Books is proud to present
a beautiful and contemporary new look
for Love Inspired!

HEARTWARMING INSPIRATIONAL ROMANCE

Love Inspired®

As always, Love Inspired delivers
endearing romances full of hope, faith and love.

Beginning January 2003
look for these titles
and three more each month
at your favorite retail outlet.

Steeple
Hill®

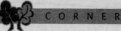

C O O P E R ' S C O R N E R

Welcome to Twin Oaks— the new B and B in Cooper's Corner. Some come for pleasure, others for passion—and one to set things straight...

Coming in January 2003... ACCIDENTAL FAMILY by Kristin Gabriel

Check-in: When former TV soap star Rowena Dahl's biological clock started ticking, she opted to get pregnant at a fertility clinic. Unfortunately, she got the wrong sperm!

Checkout: Publisher Alan Rand was outraged that a daytime diva was having *his* baby. But he soon realized that he wanted Rowena as much as he wanted their child.

HARLEQUIN®

Makes any time special®

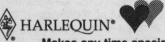

**Start the New Year off regally with
a two-book duo from**

*A runaway prince and his horse-wrangling
lookalike confuse and confound
the citizens of Ranger Springs, Texas, in*

♛A ROYAL
TWIST

by

Victoria Chancellor

Rodeo star Hank McCauley just happened to be a dead ringer
for His Royal Highness Prince Alexi of Belegovia—who had just
taken off from his tour of Texas with a spirited, sexy waitress.
Now, Hank must be persuaded by the very prim-and-proper
Lady Gwendolyn Reed to pose as the prince until the lost leader
is found. But could she turn the cowpoke into a Prince
Charming? And could Hank persuade Lady "Wendy" to let
down her barriers so that he could have her, body and soul?

Don't miss:

THE PRINCE'S COWBOY DOUBLE

January 2003

Then read Prince Alexi's story in:

THE PRINCE'S TEXAS BRIDE

February 2003

Available at your favorite retail outlet.

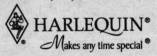